*Stacy Gardenas
announces the early arrival
of her son, Billy.
A surprised
Gareth Clelland
assisted in the delivery.
Mother and Baby
are doing fine—
and hoping to get a
father real soon!*

Dear Reader,

Take one married mom, add a surprise night of passion with her almost ex-husband, and what do you get? *Welcome Home, Daddy!* In Kristin Morgan's wonderful Romance, Rachel and Ross Murdock are now blessed with a baby on the way—and a second chance at marriage. That means Ross has only nine months to show his wife he's a FABULOUS FATHER!

Now take an any-minute-mom-to-be whose baby decides to make an appearance while she's snowbound at her handsome boss's cabin. What do you get? *An Unexpected Delivery* by Laurie Paige—a BUNDLES OF JOY book that will bring a big smile.

When one of THE BAKER BROOD hires a sexy detective to find her missing brother, she never expects to find herself walking down the aisle in Carla Cassidy's *An Impromptu Proposal.*

What's a single daddy to do when he falls for a woman with no memory? What if she's another man's wife—or another child's mother? Find out in Carol Grace's *The Rancher and the Lost Bride.*

Lynn Bulock's *And Mommy Makes Three* tells the tale of a little boy who wants a mom—and finds one in the "Story Lady" at the local library. Problem is, Dad isn't looking for a new Mrs.!

In Elizabeth Krueger's *Family Mine,* a very eligible bachelor returns to town, prepared to make an honest woman out of a single mother—but she has other ideas for him....

Finally, take six irresistible, emotional love stories by six terrific authors—and what do you get? Silhouette Romance— every month!

Enjoy every last one,

Melissa Senate
Senior Editor

Please address questions and book requests to:
Silhouette Reader Service
U.S.: 3010 Walden Ave., P.O. Box 1325, Buffalo, NY 14269
Canadian: P.O. Box 609, Fort Erie, Ont. L2A 5X3

AN UNEXPECTED DELIVERY

Laurie Paige

Silhouette

R O M A N C E™

Published by Silhouette Books

America's Publisher of Contemporary Romance

In honor of the two Graces—Emma and Katharine.
Welcome to the world!

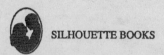 SILHOUETTE BOOKS

ISBN 0-373-19151-0

AN UNEXPECTED DELIVERY

Copyright © 1996 by Olivia M. Hall

Printed in U.S.A.

LAURIE PAIGE

was recently presented with the *Affaire de Coeur* Readers' Choice Silver Pen Award for Favorite Contemporary Author. In addition, she was a 1994 Romance Writers of America RITA finalist for Best Traditional Romance for her book *Sally's Beau*. She reports romance is blooming in her part of Northern California. With the birth of her second grandson, she finds herself madly in love with three wonderful males—"all hero material." So far, her husband hasn't complained about the other men in her life.

Bundles of Joy

Dear Reader,

All right, I confess—I'm bananas about babies. I'm not a pushover, mind you. But, well, since my grandsons were born, I must admit I look at all babies differently. For instance, that cute little gal with the dimple in one cheek and mischief in her big, brown eyes that I saw at the grocery this morning? …perfect for my three-year-old grandson. I asked her mother to give me a call in about twenty years or so.

As for Kevin, the toddler, I've already got Melissa picked out for him. She lives four houses up the street from me and is a month younger than he is. Imagine the most perfect doll with the bluest eyes and blackest hair you ever yearned for as a child. That's Melissa.

Well, enough on my grandsons' love life. Let's see, where was I? Oh, yes, the heroine is having a baby and the hero has to deliver it….

Sincerely,

Laurie Paige

Chapter One

"Yes. Yes, I'll take care of it," Stacy Gardenas said into the telephone. She finished writing her boss's directions to his country house on a notepad.

"Repeat that," he ordered.

"Take 66 west to 81," she read from her notes. "North on 81 to the first exit. Go west. Take the second right turn onto Pine Valley Road. Look for a paved lane on the left side of the road two and half miles from the turnoff."

"Okay, you got it. Tell the courier to watch for the left turn. It's tricky. Travel time will be an hour and a half. Call me back if you run into trouble."

"I'll make arrangements as soon as we hang up."

"I suppose my partner has long departed?"

Stacy grinned, but when she spoke, her tone was neutral. "Yes. He called Shirl and said he wouldn't be back today. The case was settled out of court."

"Out of court," Gareth Clelland repeated. "I'll be damned. For how much?"

She gave him the details.

"I suppose he's going to take tomorrow off, too." His voice, a baritone-bass, vibrated through the wire like the low murmur of the cello in one of Mozart's melodies. It was a voice that reflected its owner—quiet, confident and self-contained.

"Tomorrow is Friday," she answered. "And Monday is a holiday, Presidents' Day."

"Damn, I'd forgotten." There was a brief silence. "You may as well close the office after the courier picks up the package. You can take tomorrow off, too. Shirl can cover the phones."

"Right. And thank you for the time off." She waited for further instructions, pencil poised, her mind focused. Gareth didn't like to repeat himself.

"That's all, I think. It's 1:35. I'll expect the package by 3:30."

She checked her watch and adjusted it forward five minutes to match his. "I'll get right on it."

"Okay. I'll see you Tuesday then."

"Have a nice weekend," she said before he hung up.

Maybe it was mule-headedness on her part, but she persisted in inserting a few basic pleasantries into their conversations. Her taciturn employer wasted few words on amenities. She got a hello in the morning and a goodbye at night and very little in between. She added the extras.

He hesitated before replying, "Yeah. You, too."

The line echoed the faint click when he hung up. She grinned. Her niceties always seemed to surprise him and disrupt his thought processes. Well, he needed them jarred loose once in a while. All work and no play, blah, blah, blah...

She called the courier service. Then another. And another. They were booked solid. "All the gov'ment officials in D.C. are trying to clear their desks and head out of town for the long weekend,'' one of the dispatchers explained.

A common saying in the nation's capital—when government officials got a day off, they took another one to rest up for it.

She replaced the phone in its cradle and stretched her aching back. It had been hurting from the time she woke up that morning. She must have slept wrong. Or maybe it was the fact that she was eight months pregnant and counting.

Rising, she went into Gareth's office and unlocked the file cabinet. The brief was still in the folder, right where she'd placed it the other day. She wondered about that. Her boss rarely forgot anything.

After finding the other papers he wanted, she placed them inside a courier briefcase, clicked the locks on and spun the combination cylinders. Returning to her office, she tried three other delivery services before giving up.

She pondered the situation. She could deliver the documents herself since she didn't have anything pressing to do. Besides, she loved long drives in the country, and she was restless.

Grabbing her coat, purse and the briefcase, she went into the outer office to tell the secretary her plans.

"Gareth won't like your coming up there," Shirl warned.

A pebble of misgiving plunked into her stomach, adding to her discomfort. Gareth had never invited anyone to his pied-à-terre at the northern end of the Shenandoah Valley that she knew of. "Well, he can always fire me." She gave a fatalistic shrug.

She knew he wouldn't. Gareth might not like the fact that she was pregnant, but he wouldn't do anything to jeopardize her livelihood. He knew her circumstances. She turned to leave.

"Hey, wait!" the secretary called after her, "I just remembered—there's a storm moving in. The forecaster said it was going to be the biggest one this winter."

"I listened to the noon report. The snow isn't supposed to get this far south. We're only expecting freezing temperatures tonight or early tomorrow. I'll be okay. I'm going straight out there, then straight back. Besides, I'm in the ute." She waved and left the office.

The ute was a four-wheel drive, bright red sports utility. It had been her husband's pride and joy.

While she waited for the elevator to take her to the parking garage of the quiet, marble-corridored office building located on the banks of the Potomac in Arlington, Virginia, Stacy thought of Bill.

It had been a year since they'd bought the ute. Eight months since his promotion to detective on the narcotics squad. Eight months since they'd celebrated the event with candlelight, champagne and passionate delight. Eight months minus three days since he'd been killed during a stakeout at a drug house.

Six years of marriage gone. *Snap.* Just like that.

Sometimes she wondered if it would have lasted much longer. Bill had been all flicker and flash, a bright sparkle in her life after her father's death, drawing her to his radiance.

But a person needed more on a daily basis. A marriage needed a steady flame to warm it during the ups and downs of life. She'd tried to provide the balance in the relationship, but it had been difficult.

Her husband had resented her caution and had scoffed at her worries. He'd craved excitement, lived on the edge. He'd taken one risk too many.

Stacy laid a hand on her abdomen. Neither had he wanted children. She'd been stunned when she'd realized a new life had taken hold inside her—stunned and thrilled and, yes, scared, too. She was alone in the world, with no relatives to help out. A baby was a big responsibility. . . .

The elevator stopped. The cold of the unheated garage hit her when she stepped off. She pulled her coat close around her neck and hurried to the ute.

She cranked up the engine, then eased out of the garage and into the flow of traffic heading to and from the Pentagon, which was farther down the road. In a few more minutes, she was on the highway, breezing along at sixty-five miles per hour. She loved leisurely drives in this part of the country.

The Allegheny Mountains. The Shenandoah Valley. The Rappahannock River. The Appalachian Trail.

Having been born in Wyoming, which was relatively new as a state, she was constantly amazed at being in the very heart of American colonial history. She'd toured all the battle sites, the winter quarters of Washington's ragtag army and the homes of the first Americans when she'd moved to the area to live with her handsome new husband. They'd been twenty-two. So full of hopes and dreams . . .

A sigh worked its way past her lips. At twenty-eight, she had few dreams left to nourish an empty heart. The ones that remained were centered on the coming child.

A gust of wind shook the truck. It snarled at the trees along the side of the road, whipping them back and forth without mercy. Dark clouds hunkered over the terrain.

She wondered if the weatherman had called it right when he said the storm was going to miss them.

Thirty minutes later, she found out.

The first snowflakes hit her windshield as if they'd been dumped from a bucket. They were big and fluffy, shattering against the glass in silent explosions. She flipped the wipers on for intermittent swipes across the windshield.

A few minutes after that, she turned them on faster. The flakes were smaller now, but falling at a furious rate. However, it had barely coated the shoulders of the road. The steady flow of traffic prevented it from collecting on the pavement.

She relaxed and turned on the radio to listen to music and maybe catch a weather update. A little snow was nothing to worry about. The ute had tires with heavy-duty treads.

An hour and twenty minutes later, she swept around the curve onto the next highway and headed north. Taking the first exit, she was pleased at the good pace she was maintaining.

Humming along with a popular tune on the radio, she thought of what she would do with the extra time that weekend. Clean house in the morning, then finish painting the secondhand crib she'd bought and sanded down to the bare wood. She wanted to be sure there wasn't any lead paint around her baby.

She squirmed in the seat and tried to find a comfortable position. It wasn't possible.

A road led off to the right. Good. That was the first turn. She was supposed to take the second. Peering down the little-used road through the snow, she wondered how far it was.

Ten minutes later, she turned right at the intersection.

She slowed to a safe speed. The road was not only winding, it was rough. The county needed to repave it before the potholes and the creeping grass and vines completely overran the blacktop.

In fact, she might write them a letter suggesting it, she decided, after dodging one hole and hitting another, less visible one. She groaned as pain jolted up her back.

Her pace was now ten miles per hour. The road wound its way up into the hills, narrowing until it was only one lane wide. She hadn't spotted any roads going off it.

She risked a quick glance at her notes. Two and a half miles, then there should have been a paved lane to the left. He'd said the left turn was tricky. She wondered what, exactly, that had meant.

Surely she'd driven more than two and a half miles. She hadn't seen one road, either to the left or right. This had to be the wrong one. She'd better look for a place to turn around.

That was easier said than done. With the road clinging to the side of a steep hill, she didn't come across one place she considered wide enough to turn the ute. She drove on.

The snow was still coming fast and thick. An inch or more had built up on the road. Along the side, the wind piled it into drifts. Didn't anyone live on this godforsaken mountain?

Growing desperate at finding a turning point, she finally chose a wide spot at a ninety-degree curve and stopped.

She pulled close to the edge, put the truck in four-wheel drive and backed up against the slope of the bank. Then she eased forward, turning the wheels as far as they would go. After three such maneuvers, she faced downhill.

She struggled out of her coat and wiped the sweat from her face. Taking a calming breath, she eased off the brakes and headed down. The snow obliterated the tire tracks within a few feet. No one on the highway would notice where she'd turned off and taken the wrong road.

It occurred to her that she should have called Gareth and told him she would be bringing the documents he wanted.

The tires skidded sideways through the snow as she rounded a turn. She cut the wheel the other way, which was toward the tree-lined cliff that edged the road. The ute came out of the skid. She steered into the curve again and prayed the tires would hold.

They did.

Sweat popped out and dried on her skin, making her feel both clammy and cold. The temperature was certainly dropping. She could vouch for that. And the storm was growing worse.

Finally, she came to the intersection. She glanced at her watch and groaned aloud. She'd spent over two hours on this trip and hadn't reached her destination yet. Perhaps she should go home while the road was still navigable....

A strange pain gripped her. It started as a clenching sensation in her lower back, then swept around to embrace her. She gasped and clutched one arm across her abdomen.

It was almost a minute before it let up.

She sat there, dazed by the attack. That's what it had felt like—as if something had grabbed her body and put a Vise-Grip on it, pulling tighter and tighter.

Her hands trembled as she resumed her trip. A mile down the road, she realized she needed to stop again.

Pressing the brakes hard, she slithered on the fresh snow. She let up on the pedal and pumped it. She came to a stop in the middle of the road and briefly worried about traffic.

Since there wasn't another set of tracks of any kind to be seen, she didn't think getting run over was going to be a big problem. Laying her head against the back of the seat, she clasped both hands across her body and held on while another contraction squeezed her like a ripe orange.

A moan broke through her control. The pain was worse this time. She felt heavy and strung out when it was over.

One thing she knew, she had to find the cabin. If this wasn't Braxton Hicks contractions, as Dr. Kate called false labor, then she needed help. She drove on.

Just when she was ready to give up to despair, she spied a road sign. Pine Valley Road. Thank heavens.

Gareth's house was on a paved lane two and a half miles from there. She turned, then set the trip mileage indicator to zero and drove down the county road, relieved to be nearing the end of this treacherous journey.

A few minutes later, she came upon a curve in the road that curled downhill. Glancing at the trip indicator, she saw she'd gone the required distance. She looked for the left turn.

Gareth had been right. It was a tricky turn. The lane wasn't visible until she was almost past the entrance. She swerved sharply in surprise when she realized this was it and automatically hit the brake pedal.

For a second, she thought she was going to make it. She should have known better. Fate was working against her.

The back tires broke loose first. Then the front. The truck slid gracefully off the road into a shallow ditch like an ice skater performing a trick. With a jarring *thump*, the truck hit a telephone pole and came to rest.

Stacy couldn't move. She gripped the steering wheel as another pain shot through her. She tried to remember how she was supposed to breathe, but the instructions went completely out of her mind. Instead, she held on and waited for it to be over.

One minute and twenty seconds. Was that too long for false labor? It couldn't be. She couldn't be having a baby a month early out here on some road in the middle of no-where during a raging blizzard. She couldn't!

She took her foot off the brake pedal and eased down on the gas very gently. The truck jumped a bit but it didn't move forward. She bit her lip and tried again. The tires spun uselessly, unable to get a grip in the snow.

Getting out, she pulled on her coat and gloves, then bent to inspect the problem. Her heart sank. The truck was buried in mud and snow right up to the axle.

Well, one good thing—she knew she was at the right place. The truck had clipped another post as it cavorted across the road and into the ditch. A mailbox lay on its side, half buried in the snow. G. Clelland was painted on it in block letters.

Stacy stood the post up and propped the mailbox on it. Using a rock, she pounded the nail down into the wood to hold it on. To her delight, the post stayed upright when she finished.

She glanced down at her clothes. At least she had on warm wool flannel slacks. She kept snow boots in the truck that she could pull on over her flats. She would walk to Gareth's place.

From there, she could call a tow truck to get her out. She tugged her boots on, pulled a toboggan hat down over her ears, buttoned her coat to her chin and slung her purse over one shoulder. With the briefcase in one hand, she locked the truck and started down the road. With her luck, his house was probably located ten miles from the begin-ning of the lane.

Fifteen minutes later, she was afraid she'd been more right than she wanted to be. Not a house in sight.

What she wouldn't give to see a friendly chimney send-ing up a plume of smoke like a welcoming signal.

She stopped and placed her hands on her knees. From a half crouch, she rocked through another contraction. If she was in labor, walking was supposed to move things along faster.

Poor baby. He might be born in a snow bank if his mama's luck continued the way it had started. She remembered a saying—if it weren't for bad luck, I'd have no luck at all.

She laughed. The sound was high and thin. She worried that she was succumbing to hysteria. She had to keep her head. Her child depended on her.

Who could she depend on? No one. But she'd be okay. She just had to keep walking...keep walking....

The words echoed through her brain with each step. She put one foot in front of the other and kept it up. She remembered to watch for a house. To walk right past the place would be really stupid...even more than making the journey in the first place.

The scent of wood smoke caught her attention. She paused and sniffed the wind like a deer trying to find its way.

The snow fell all around her and the pine trees with little rustling noises. Taffeta rubbing against taffeta. Her breath was the only other sound.

She imagined being alone, the last person in the entire world. The silence of the woods made it too real. She shivered and hurried on, following the scent of wood smoke.

Finally she came into a clearing. And there was the house. She stopped, her mouth agape.

It wasn't a simple cabin by any means. Glass panels soared upward to form a spire at the highest peak of the roof. A huge wooden door, surely belonging to some medieval castle, stood below the second-story wall of glass.

The lower floor of the building was made of stone, the upper of wooden beams.

Smoke wafted from a stone chimney in lazy curls of gray-white, barely visible against the falling snow.

She walked up the steps and thumped the brass knocker in the middle of the massive door. Five seconds later, the door opened. Her boss stared at her, his face closed and remote.

"Hi," she said spritely. "Sorry to be late."

She handed the briefcase over, then bent forward and clutched her thighs as another pain tightened around her.

"What is it?" he demanded, definitely in a foul mood.

With her teeth clenched, it was hard to speak. "Baby," she said. "I think it's coming."

"God in heaven," he muttered and set the briefcase down.

"Yeah. He's wise to stay in. It's a terrible night."

Under the circumstances, she didn't think it was that bad a joke. However, the Great Stone Face didn't crack a smile. The pain eased. She straightened slowly, her legs shaky from strain.

Gareth swept her into his arms and carried her inside like a hero in a melodrama. Too shocked to protest this odd behavior, she rested her cheek against his shoulder. His warmth made her realize how cold she was, his eyes how unwelcome.

"I'll just rest a minute, then I'll be going," she said.

He kicked the door closed, his face grim as death.

Chapter Two

Gareth muttered a curse, then set his teeth together and held back the rest of the words.

Why him?

There was no answer. There never was. Fate waved its evil hand and catastrophe struck. Humans had no say in the matter, nor any way to guard themselves against it. He cursed again.

Then wished he hadn't.

His assistant gazed up at him. Her eyes, usually the color of milk chocolate, were wells of darkness, reflecting pain and... Could that be fear he saw in the depths?

He frowned, finding it difficult to associate her with fear. She had such a dauntless spirit.

Surprised, he wondered where that thought had come from. If asked, he'd have said his assistant was competent, neat and quiet around the office. Other than those bare facts, he knew next to nothing about her.

That wasn't true. He'd stood beside her at her husband's funeral, ready to catch her if she fainted or to restrain her if she tried to throw herself into the grave. Neither of those heroic deeds had been necessary.

She'd been quiet then, too, and stoic in the face of the tragedy. She'd taken the standard three days off, then quietly returned to work and got on with it.

Only one time had he witnessed uncontrolled emotion in her. That was when her doctor had called to confirm the pregnancy. He'd hung up the phone on a client and had run into her office, thinking something terrible had happened when he'd heard her initial shriek. Then he'd realized she was laughing, sort of hysterically, but it was laughter.

"I'm pregnant," she'd cried, her eyes shining. She'd whooped with excitement. "Pregnant! Oh, God, pregnant!"

He'd been in no doubt about her joy then. He studied her face. She didn't look so happy at the moment.

The bit of lipstick that remained on her mouth contrasted starkly with the pallor of her usually tawny complexion. He couldn't figure it out. What the hell was she doing here?

She moved her head against his shoulder. A strand of hair, damp with snow, caught on the beard he hadn't bothered to shave in a couple of days. A spicy scent drifted up to him, one of vanilla and cinnamon with a hint of lemon and the sweetness of honey. He inhaled, drawing the fragrance deep into his lungs.

A sound, not quite a groan, not quite a sigh, escaped her parted lips. A funny sensation ran through his chest, a sort of tightening or clenching feeling.

Striding up the stairs, he became aware of how delicately her body curved against his, how weightless she seemed compared to his much larger mass, although he knew she was an average-size woman, five feet five inches, nicely rounded.

And pregnant, he reminded himself as his body stirred, shocking him with the tingling demands of passion.

In his room, he laid her on the king-size bed and bent to take her boots off. She put out a hand and stopped him.

"Wait," she said, then gave a little gasp.

Her fingers curled around his hand, squeezing harder and harder as she rode out the spasm. Her teeth sank into her bottom lip as she held back any sounds of distress.

Sweat poured out all over his body. His own muscles clenched involuntarily, straining with her effort to expel the child from her body.

"We need an ambulance," he muttered.

"There isn't time." She released the breath she'd held and let go of his hand.

Standing, she removed her hat and coat and handed them to him. He tossed them over the desk chair in the corner.

She wore brown slacks with a long-sleeved maternity top in a pastel pink. A multicolored scarf encircled her neck and was held in place with a dragon pin on the shoulder of her blouse.

"Do you have a rubber mat?" she asked.

A strange question. "There might be a plastic sheet left from some painting I did last summer."

"Better get it and put it on the bed. And an extra sheet. And towels."

"Right."

Relieved at having something to do, he hurried out of the room and down the stairs. He found the large piece of plastic he'd used as a drop cloth to catch paint splatters. Pausing at the counter, he glanced at the stairs, then picked up the phone. They needed help. He didn't know how to deliver a baby.

There was no dial tone. He clicked the button several times and got nothing besides the static *hiss* of an empty line.

He glared at the instrument.

A noise from upstairs forced him to give up on the phone for the moment. He bounded up the steps three at a time.

At the door to his bedroom, he stopped. His executive assistant was down to her skivvies and about to take those off.

Need, heavy and urgent, jolted through his nether regions. He glanced down at his jeans as if discovering a new part of himself. Clearing his throat, he entered the room.

Her shoes and snow boots were lined up like toy soldiers at attention against the wall. Her slacks were folded and placed on the chair where he'd thrown her coat and hat. These, too, were neatly arranged.

"Uhnn."

The groan brought his eyes back to her. Her blouse ballooned around her as she bent and clutched her thighs.

He stared, half in fascination, half in horror, as her body tightened around her abdomen. The involuntary hardening of the muscles reminded him of a charley horse he'd once had in the calf of his leg. It had hurt like hell. He remembered that, too.

Another part of him—a part he couldn't seem to control—noticed how smooth and shapely her legs were.

The blood throbbed deep in his body. He couldn't understand it—getting all hot and bothered because a woman was in his bedroom. A woman about to have a child, at that. Weird.

He called himself a name, but couldn't stop the sensations that assailed him. Having a baby reminded him of the process of making one. A very pleasant process, if he remembered correctly, he cynically remarked to his alert libido.

"Help me," she said on a gasp.

He forced his mind back to the problem at hand, a much more serious one than his. "How? What should I do?"

"Need to...sit down."

He lifted her as gently as he could and placed her on the bed. She began breathing in quick pants.

"Easy," he said. He hunkered down in front of her and took her hands. "Slow and easy. Take a deep breath. Let it out, nice and easy. That's the way."

Gradually she eased her hold on him, then released him. "We need to fix the bed." Twin lines grooved the space between her eyebrows. She sighed as if weary beyond bearing.

"Right." He made her sit in a chair while he pushed the top sheet to the foot of the bed, then spread the plastic over the bottom sheet. He covered it with the clean one.

"Do you have an iron?" she asked.

"A what?"

"An iron. To iron the sheet. It kills germs."

"Oh." He thought there might be one in the kitchen. "Be right back." Like a marathon racer, he sped to the kitchen and returned. "Got it."

He felt as if he'd achieved some great feat and should be rewarded with a crown of laurel leaves.

She was all business. "Plug it in and run it over the sheet. Turn it on high."

He followed the orders as if his life depended on it.

Hers might.

He shied from that thought. Women had babies all the time, all over the world, without medical help.

They also died. Sometimes with the best medical treatment in the world. He shook his head, negating that worry. There was no time for anything but the crisis at hand.

"How are you feeling?" he asked.

"Not too good." She removed the pin and scarf, fastened the pin back on the material and laid it on his dresser. "I'm sorry about this. I never dreamed ... It was just ... I was so restless and I thought ... Anyway, I'm terribly sorry."

He waved her apology aside. "What are you doing here?"

"There was no courier available. I decided a drive would be nice. It's lovely here in the mountains. In the city, you forget they're so close."

"Yeah. Not like Wyoming where you can go for seconds and not see a mountain." He was pleased when she smiled at his joke.

"Do you have a T-shirt I could wear? Extra large, if you have one."

"Sure." He retrieved one from a drawer.

After handing it to her, he stood a couple of feet away, waiting for her next instruction. It occurred to him that in this situation she would have to call all the shots.

"Uh, would you mind?" she asked.

It took him a second, but he finally caught on. She didn't want him to watch her remove her blouse. Heat ran under his skin, and he felt like a kid caught spying on a pretty neighbor. He spun around so his back was to her.

But in his mental vision, he could see her, looking fragile and incredibly beautiful. He wondered why he'd never noticed the curve of her lip, the shape of her nose, the indentation of her chin that wasn't quite a dimple, during all the months they'd worked together. A year, and he'd never looked at her?

"Okay," she said.

When he turned, he found her in bed with his T-shirt on. She'd pushed the pillows into a pile against the headboard and spread the top sheet over her. Her knees were drawn up, making a tent so he couldn't see her pumpkin shape. Her hair was in a tangle of curls on his pillow.

The strangest thing happened. For an instant, no more than the time between one heartbeat and the next, it seemed perfectly right that he should crawl into bed and make love to her. He clenched his fists, fighting the insane urge that was so strong, he feared he'd do it before he could stop himself.

"I really am sorry to trouble you," she apologized again. Her gaze slid away from his. He realized she was embarrassed.

He could hardly rail at her for coming out here in her condition, not at the moment. Adopting a light tone, he gave a snort of sardonic laughter. "I'm a little put out about it myself."

"I think you'd better call that ambulance," she advised, closing her eyes and pressing against the pillows. A fierce frown turned her lightly spoken request into a serious one. He realized she was having another pain.

How long since the last one? Wasn't someone supposed to time them or something? Yeah, *he* was that someone.

She looked at him. Her eyes had the depth, the texture of velvet. He could lie down in them and... Fear flickered through those dark chocolate depths.

He swallowed and concentrated. "The phone's out. I tried, but there's no dial tone." He strode to the desk and picked up the extension. "Still no luck." He managed to keep the worry out of his voice. He'd have to be the calm one here.

"Probably my fault. The truck hit the telephone pole when it went into the ditch, also the mailbox. But I fixed it. Where's your cellular phone?"

"At my apartment. I forgot it." He couldn't believe he'd understood her right. "You went off the road?"

But she couldn't answer. Her hand reached out. He caught it in his. Sitting beside her, he held both her hands as the gripping thrust of her body racked through them both.

The sweat was standing on his brow as much as hers when it was over. "That was a long one," she informed him.

"Yeah, I know." He glanced at the alarm clock. Over a minute and a half. *God help them.*

"You'll need scissors and thread," she told him, wiping at her face with a towel. She handed him one of the extras he'd brought in at her request. "Clean them with alcohol. Or boiling water will do, just like in the movies." She smiled.

Any minute now, he'd wake with this strange, restless night behind him. He glanced at the window. Night had fallen, but it was hours before dawn. This was no dream.

Grim reality took over. This was really going to happen. Stacy, the quiet, the competent, was going to have a baby. In his home. In his bed.

"Anything else?" he asked.

She flashed that smile again, a brave smile. He knew it was a facade, and that she did it for him. That gave him another odd jolt inside.

"Iron a towel to wrap the baby in. Billy," she added. "To wrap Billy in."

"Billy," he repeated. The baby's father had been Bill, a nickname for William. He nodded and set about doing the tasks.

When everything was clean and laid out to her satisfaction, he sat on the bed beside her. "Take my hands," he offered when he saw the frown start on her forehead.

She grabbed hold of him as if she'd never let go. She breathed deeply, then started panting. She released him and pulled her knees toward her chest.

"Ohh," she moaned softly. She drew a deep breath and held it. And held it. And held it.

He knelt beside the bed and checked the progress. "I see it," he told her. He swallowed hard as a knot formed in his throat. Then there was no time for thoughts or feelings.

"Can you . . . see his head?" she asked, panting again.

"Uh, yes." He thought it was the head. Then, "Yes, yes, it is. It's coming. Here it comes."

She moaned and strained as hard as she could.

"That's it," he said. Excitement crept into his voice. "You're doing good. The head is out. It's facing backward."

She breathed deeply, relaxing. "I think that's how it should be. Make sure the cord isn't around his neck."

"No, it isn't. I don't see it."

"Okay."

Relief swept over him. He didn't know what was supposed to happen next. She seemed to be resting.

Minutes ticked past. He noticed how loud silence could be. The sighing of the wind, the whisper of snow at the windows, the creaks of the house reminded him of the isolation of the place.

Stacy made a slight sound. He saw the tightening of her abdomen and knew she was going into another contraction. He looked up and met her eyes.

Something invisible reached out and grabbed him, dipping right into his soul. Threads of light wove around them, drawing them tighter and tighter together. He waited, spellbound by this phenomenon that was beyond his previous experience.

Stacy shifted restlessly. She clutched at the sheets and breathed deeply, then began panting.

He wanted to kiss her. "It's okay," he murmured.

She made another giant push and the child was born, sliding into his hands like a wet watermelon seed. The baby gave an indignant yell, then settled into a mewling cry.

"A boy!" he said. "It's a boy! By damn, we did it!"

"Let me see him."

He held the baby up. "Everything's there. Fingers, toes. Eyes, ears. All the right parts in all the right places." He was grinning like an idiot.

She smiled, too. "Now finish," she told him.

"Right." He managed to sever the cord without fainting, although he'd never be fooled into thinking men were the stronger sex again. Stacy told him everything to do.

"Give him to me," she requested when it was over. She lay against the pillows looking pale and beautiful.

Gareth laid the baby in her waiting arms. He removed the used towels and the sheet, replacing them with fresh ones. Then he leaned over her and the baby. He brushed the hair from her temples with fingers that still trembled ever so little.

"You are one of the bravest people I've ever met," he said in reverent tones. His heart felt too big for his chest.

Her eyes widened.

He left before she could reply. After cleaning up and starting the washing machine, he tried the phone again. Still no luck. He went up the stairs.

Stacy had her eyes closed. The baby nestled beside her, wrapped in the towel he'd ironed. He needed to fashion a diaper for him, but for right now, he'd let them rest.

Fatigue washed over him. He went to the glass panels that formed one wall of the room. It was separated from the outer wall of windows by a sun room, designed to collect solar heat during the day and radiate it into the house at night.

Opening the door silently, he crossed the heat-absorbing tiles and stood by the outside windows. The snow still fell. It was eight inches deep, more in the drifts. The snowplow wouldn't get through until Monday or Tuesday.

He forced his mind to practical matters. He had plenty of food, even with unexpected guests....

God, he couldn't believe he'd delivered a baby, one that seemed to be okay. So many things could have gone wrong.

Blackness pushed out of his soul, engulfing him.

Gripping the window frame, he quit fighting and let the memories wash over him, unable to hold them back any longer.

Three years ago, he'd rushed to a hospital on an emergency. His fiancée had been in an accident—a drunken driver had swerved into her lane going almost one hundred miles an hour.

"Where is she?" he'd asked, spotting the doctor, also a friend, who'd called him with the news.

The doctor had gestured toward the Intensive Care Unit. "She's waiting for you."

It wasn't until later that he'd understood what his friend had meant—that Ginny had waited until he could hold her one last time. One last kiss. A few desperate murmured words.

And then she was gone.

One week before their wedding. She'd been two months pregnant with their child.

Guilt and despair pummeled him. Her death had been his fault. He'd called her while in flight and asked her to meet his plane. They'd been apart a whole week. His desire to see her had overcome common sense.

He beat the anger and other useless emotions back by force of will. What was gone, was gone. He'd survived. He hadn't wanted to, but he had.

He shook his head, wondering why he was remembering the past at this moment when he'd been able to avoid it for three years.

Remembering was no good. It served no purpose. He had other things to do. Like check on Stacy's truck to see what kind of mess she'd gotten herself into.

Returning to the bedroom, he stood there watching the new mother and her child sleep. A chasm opened in him, like a sealed vault whose lock had been breached. Stacy and her son somehow exposed the emptiness that dwelled inside him. He didn't like it. Laid bare, the void hurt like a raw nerve.

He pushed the thought aside. Stacy was his assistant, well educated and trained to his way of doing things. He'd been planning on talking to her about studying to be a paralegal. She had the brains for it and the self-discipline. The pregnancy had halted his ideas on that.

The birth of the child changed things, too. He just didn't know how yet. He didn't want to think about it. After this incident was over, he wouldn't have to see the baby again. Stacy had a nursery school lined up.

He'd give her some time off, all she needed. When she returned, everything would be normal again.

If it wasn't, he'd help her find another job.

* * *

Stacy woke with a start. The baby gave a tiny, forlorn cry that wrenched her heart. "There, now. You're fine. We're both okay. Thanks to Gareth," she added.

Her boss might never recover from the shock of delivering a baby—he'd looked pretty green there at the end—but he'd been wonderful during the ordeal.

She sighed and moved cautiously. To her surprise, she didn't feel sore. That was one fast delivery. From the time she'd felt the first real contraction until the birth had been less than two hours.

"Well, I'm not sure what comes next, but perhaps we'd better try feeding you," she said to the baby. She pushed upright against the pillows and fumbled with the lamp until she found the switch. Soft light illuminated the large bedroom.

Outside the windows—a double set, she saw, with a room between them—night had settled in. Snowflakes bounced off the glass panels and piled up on the outer ledge.

Glancing at the bedside clock, she discovered it was only a few minutes after eight. She thought she'd arrived around five, but she wasn't sure. Time had ceased to have meaning during that last hour or so.

She laid the baby down and tucked the T-shirt under the strap of her maternity bra. She unhooked the flap and the cup peeled down, exposing her breast. She lifted the baby and rubbed his rosebud mouth against the nipple.

That seemed to excite him. He opened his eyes and bobbed his head around frantically. She guided him in the right direction. He latched on like a pit bull.

"Ouch!" she exclaimed, jerking against the pillows.

He lost his hold and let out a wail. She helped him find the nipple again. This time she was prepared and didn't move when he tugged.

Odd sensations shot off into her chest, sort of painful, but not entirely. The baby lost his hold. Again they went through the finding and latching on procedure. This happened several times until he dozed off.

She wondered if he'd gotten anything. She tried squeezing to see if anything came out. Nothing did.

When she heard footsteps in the hall, she yanked the sheet over her, baby and all, while she fumbled beneath it to close the bra clasp and pull down the T-shirt.

Gareth entered the room as the baby let out a wail. He checked on the threshold, then entered the room. "Is he all right?" he asked.

"Yes." She laid the baby on her tummy, which felt so odd in its newly flattened state, and struggled with the bra under the cover. The baby wailed louder.

"What are you doing?" Gareth frowned at her warily.

Heat flowed up her neck into her face. It was rather ridiculous to be embarrassed at this late date after what she'd put him through that afternoon, but she couldn't help it.

"Well, uh," she said, stalling while waiting for a brilliant reply to pop into her mind.

"What's wrong with the boy?" He leaned over her, menacing in his bigness.

He was a powerfully built man, over six feet tall, with shoulders like a football player in full uniform. His hands and feet were proportionately large. He hadn't shaved that morning and a dark stubble swept around his strong jawline, giving him the ominous appearance of a tramp.

His jeans, scuffed boots and blue corduroy shirt, worn out at the elbows, added to this impression. His dark hair was tousled. It was a contrast to his usual urbane appearance.

There was one thing that wasn't different from what he was like was at the office. His gray eyes still looked directly at a person as if he could see right to the back of the skull.

Her gaze went to his hands, now tensed at his sides. They were big, too. And, unlike the hard gaze he turned on her, they were gentle.

Those hands had trembled when he'd tied and cut the cord, then positioned a plastic bowl for the afterbirth as she'd directed. When he'd held the baby up so she could see that her child was all right, they had been gentle—large, capable and so very, very gentle. She loved his hands.

"Stacy," he snapped.

She blinked up at him. She dropped the sheet and brought the child up to her shoulder. "He's fine. I was trying to feed him, but he keeps going to sleep. I'm not sure if he got anything to eat or not."

All at once, she felt helpless and stupid. What did she know about raising a child? Nothing.

She'd had no brothers or sisters. Her mother had died a long time ago, her father during her junior year in college. She was the only child of two only children. No aunts, uncles or cousins. She'd never been around babies in any capacity, had never earned money baby-sitting....

A wet warmth spread over her stomach. "Oh," she said.

Gareth followed her gaze. "I'll find something for a diaper." He left the room practically at a run.

Poor man, he was probably scared to death something terrible was going to happen. As if helping birth a baby wasn't terrible enough for a hardened bachelor like him.

She giggled. She couldn't help it. It was too funny. Gareth Clelland, hotshot legal eagle, one of the foremost attorneys in the country who argued cases in front of the Supreme Court, was stuck in a cabin with a nervous new mother and a crying infant, acting as midwife and nanny.

When he returned, looking grim and remote, she burst into fresh giggles. This was something to write about, if she'd had anyone to write to, which she didn't.

"Stop it," he ordered.

She wiped the smile off. "Yes, sir," she returned smartly. Then she giggled again.

"Are you hysterical?" he asked in a milder tone.

Taking a firm hold on her runaway emotions, she shook her head. "Sorry. It struck me as funny—you a high-powered attorney having to play nursemaid."

He gave her a quizzical glance. One dark eyebrow rose in sardonic humor. When he grinned, lines appeared at the corners of his eyes. "Yeah, it's a barrel of laughs."

She loved his smile. Even if it was laced with cynicism, it appeared genuine, not like the social ones she'd seen at the office. "I'm also embarrassed."

"You needn't be." He laid several dish towels on the bed, plus a piece of plastic cut from a garbage bag. "I thought you could use these." He reached into his pocket and laid two safety pins beside the dish towel.

"Good." She unwrapped the baby, dried him, then folded the makeshift diaper and plastic around him and pinned them in place.

Gareth ironed a dry towel and brought it to her. She wrapped the baby in the terry cloth bunting. "I don't think you need to iron the towels anymore."

He unplugged the iron. For a second he didn't say anything, then he nodded. "Are you hungry?"

She considered. "I don't know. I'm still sort of numb...." She felt the blush start again. "I mean, after all that's happened and everything. I really haven't thought about it," she finished lamely.

His lips thinned. "I made some soup earlier today."

"Well," she said. "Multitalented—and all of them amazing." She clamped down on her runaway tongue. He was going to fire her for sure if she didn't control herself.

"I'll bring you some supper," he decided, not waiting for her to make a decision. He left the room.

Lying against the pillows, she wondered about him. He was almost forty. Why hadn't he married?

She knew he dated, mostly high society women from the capital or Virginia, where his office was located, although not regularly and no one in particular. She'd sometimes heard him make reservations or order tickets to concerts and events at Lincoln Center and places like that.

It must be pleasant to go someplace with a man like him. He could be charming when he wished. She'd heard him laughing once during a phone conversation with one of his dates. His tone had been low, deep and intimate. It had given her goose bumps.

That had been when she first started to work for him. For the past few months, he'd been so busy he hadn't gone out.

Or maybe he didn't make the arrangements so she could hear. Her mouth dropped open. That was it. She hadn't heard him on the phone with one of the many women interested in him since... since the funeral. Was he being considerate of her?

When a woman occasionally called him at work, he closed the door between their offices before taking the call. He must have realized seeing or hearing other couples had been painful for her for the first few months after her own loss.

Until she'd found out about the baby. Then the world had seemed bright again.

She'd point out this considerate aspect of Gareth to Shirl when she went back to work. He wasn't a heartless beast at all.

When he returned with a tray in one hand and a clean T-shirt in the other, she was composed. He placed the tray on the bed and tossed the shirt to her.

"Oh, thanks." She hadn't wanted to ask him for a dry one. She didn't know how many clothes he brought with him or kept at the mountain retreat.

Sniffing the comforting aroma of homemade chicken noodle soup, she realized she was indeed hungry. It had been a long time since lunch. She looked around for a place to lay the baby and decided the other side of the bed would have to do.

Gareth placed the tray, which was on short legs, on the floor. He went to a closet and returned with an armful of pillows. These he placed around the child on the other side of the king-size mattress, making a safe nest.

"Perfect," she said as he leaned down to set the tray across her lap.

He was very close, his face no more than six inches from hers. Smoky blue-gray color outlined his irises in a most attractive fashion, emphasizing the light gray in the middle.

For a minute he paused, holding her gaze with his while currents of some ephemeral substance wound around them. She tried to think of something to say...anything....

He straightened, breaking the strange connection, his face its usual mask of polite indifference.

She wasn't sure what had happened. If anything.

He muttered something and walked out, leaving her staring after him like a dolt.

Feeling the damp T-shirt against her, she quickly slipped it over her head and pulled on the fresh one, her mind elsewhere.

She'd read about the hormone changes and mood swings motherhood could bring during the first few days or weeks while the body got back to normal and life settled down. That must account for the knot in her throat and the clamoring of her pulse. That and the fact she'd forced her boss into a most embarrassing position by coming to his hideaway.

Pulling the tray closer, she picked up the spoon and wished she could wiggle her nose and be back at home in her own bed with this day just starting. She'd certainly change a few things about it.

The baby stirred and tried to suck his fingers. A funny feeling attacked her insides, a mixture of love and tenderness for this tiny creature given into her care.

She continued to watch him while she ate. He was the one thing she wouldn't change about the comedy of errors that had happened that day.

Realizing she was tired, she finished the chicken noodle soup. Homemade, no less. By her boss.

Wow, as Shirl would say.

She'd almost gone to sleep again when Gareth stalked into the room. "Finished?"

"Yes. That was delicious." She offered him a smile.

He didn't notice. With admirable efficiency, he removed the tray and damp T-shirt, taking them with him as he left the room.

"Wait," she called.

He turned at the door.

"Do you happen to have a cardboard box or something I can use for a cradle? I'm afraid I'll roll over on the baby if I go to sleep."

He hesitated, then nodded and left.

She wondered about that pause. A muscle had jumped in his jaw before he'd nodded. And in his eyes... She must have imagined that odd bleakness, the pain and despair.

Yes, her hormones were acting up. She was the one with the emotional upheavals, not him. She waited anxiously until she heard his footsteps on the stairs.

He strode in and set a wooden cradle on the foot of the bed. "Will this do?"

She stared at it. "Why, yes." She reached out to stroke the satin-smooth wood. "It's beautiful. Was it hand-made?"

"Yes."

"It must be an antique."

"A replica," he said and walked out as if he had an important meeting to attend and she was detaining him.

Giving a wry glance at his retreating back, she picked up the sleeping baby and held him with shy tenderness.

Gareth stalked back into the room, filling it with his masculine bigness. He placed a folded bath towel in the cradle and set it on the side of the king-size bed within arm's reach.

She laid little Billy down, then examined the cradle in detail. The sides were made from spindles, the head and foot of solid wood. An intricately carved scene of trees and grass, a flowing brook, rocks and wildflowers decorated each end piece. An owl sat on the branches of a tree, looking wise as owls were supposed to.

Why, she wondered, would a bachelor have a hand-made cradle at his hideaway in the mountains?

Looking at his closed expression, she was afraid to ask.

Chapter Three

Stacy slept fitfully during the night. So did the child. She kept the bedside lamp on so she could check on her son often during the slow hours until dawn. She tried not to think of all the things that could go wrong. Besides, it did no good to worry. A person had to face things as they happened.

Billy seemed to like the cradle. When she woke to the faint light of the cloudy morning, she found him with his eyes open, looking around as if checking out the world instead of whimpering as he'd done each time he'd stirred during the night.

"Good morning. Like what you see?" she asked, lifting him to her lap and trying another feeding.

Her nipples were sore from the latching on, losing it, then latching on again. Babies, although driven by instinct, had to learn to suckle. She hoped he caught on soon.

"Ouch, ouch, ouch," she murmured as he settled in for some serious feeding. Her breasts were engorged and rather tender. "Could you be a little easier?"

"He'll learn by the time he's twenty-one," a masculine voice predicted with a sardonic edge.

Gareth stood in the doorway, his hands thrust into his pockets. He was freshly shaved, otherwise he looked much the same as the previous day—boots, jeans, T-shirt under the same out-at-the-elbows blue corduroy shirt.

"But that'll be too late to do me any good," she groused, then realized the innuendo behind the words. Heat climbed from her breasts, up her neck and into her face.

"Yeah. Tough," he said in mock sympathy. He laid a clean supply of dish towels on the bedside table.

As an ice breaker, it wasn't much, but the good-natured heckling helped her over the initial embarrassment of facing her boss after yesterday's events.

"Did we keep you awake last night?" She thought it was time for a change in subject.

She was acutely conscious of her son making little noises at her breast as he nursed, not to mention the fact that her breast, which to her eyes resembled a huge pale melon of some strange species, was visible and that she had to hold it away from Billy's nose so he could breathe. She flattened her hand over the bulging mound to hide as much of it as possible.

"No, I slept fine."

"Where...that is, I can move to another bedroom. This one is yours."

He shrugged. "There are three bedrooms downstairs. I'm in one of them. It's quieter up here for you and... Billy."

She wondered at the pause before he said the baby's name. His eyes flicked to the child in her arms, then away. It came to her that he might not like children. Or their mothers.

"What would you like for breakfast?" he asked.

"Cereal or toast, if you have it," she said, keeping a bright note in her voice with an effort. She glanced at his hands and remembered how gentle he'd been while tending her and her son during the delivery. "Yesterday," she said impulsively, "you were magnificent, simply magnificent."

To her amazement, he flushed brick red. Her stone-faced boss was blushing?

"Yeah, well, I don't think I'll take it up as a hobby," he informed her and abruptly left.

The hard edge had returned. She looked down, disappointed. She'd imagined that moment of emotion between them.

She finished feeding Billy. He seemed to get enough for he settled into sleep immediately afterward. She placed the baby between two pillows, then eased out of bed.

Going into the bathroom, she wet a washcloth in warm water. She washed her son and changed his diaper, then laid him in the cradle. He was sound asleep.

After considering for all of two seconds, she decided to take a quick shower. Using Gareth's soap and shampoo, then his deodorant and powder and comb, she was in and out of the bathroom faster than she'd ever been in her entire life.

Little Billy slept peacefully, his puckered mouth moving as if sucking. His lips had a blistered look, but that was normal, the baby books reported.

She found a blue velour robe on the back of the bathroom door and put it on, wondering which of Gareth's female friends had given it to him. It didn't strike her as something he'd buy for himself. She slipped into her flats and went downstairs. Gareth was in the kitchen. He was scrambling eggs.

He took in her appearance in one glance, then removed two plates from the oven. He spooned out the eggs beside the sausage and toast on each plate and carried them to the table.

"Breakfast," he announced.

She sat down. He joined her after pouring coffee in thick mugs and bringing them over. She picked up her fork and started in when he did. "This is delicious," she told him. "I didn't realize how hungry I was."

"You didn't eat much last night." He stopped, then rose as if he'd thought of something. He fetched a glass and filled it with milk. He brought it to the table and placed it beside her plate. "Nursing mothers need milk," he said at her questioning glance.

"How did you know that?"

"I have a sister. She and her husband have two children."

She gaped at him in surprise. In the year she'd worked for him, he hadn't mentioned his family once. Sometimes she thought of him as an orphan like herself.

However, his parents lived in a small town about a hundred miles south of Arlington. She'd spoken with his mother a few times, taking messages regarding family celebrations and dinners, but no one else from his family had ever called.

She started to question him about them, but thought better of it. When he didn't volunteer any further information, she kept her curiosity to herself. He wasn't given to small talk, at least not with her.

Shirl knew less about him than Stacy, in spite of the other woman having been with the law firm longer. Neither of them knew what the middle initial of his name stood for.

He'd been named for one of his grandfathers, she decided. Butler. Or Buchanan. Beech. Barnett. Those were old Virginia names she'd found in the cemeteries she'd visited.

Gareth Butler Clelland. Gareth Buchanan Clelland. If he'd been named Adam, his initials would be A.B.C.

"What's so funny?"

Her unconscious smile widened into a grin. She explained about the initials.

"It's Beauregard."

"You're joking," she said before she thought.

He looked at her solemnly. Then she noticed his eyes. They were laughing at her. His mouth curled into a half smile. His expression was cynical, yes, but amused, too.

"You *are* joking."

"Don't look so surprised."

"Well, it is rather as if the Sphinx smiled," she blurted, then pressed her fingertips over her mouth. She was going to get herself fired if she didn't watch it.

Gareth could be pleasant. He had a low, sexy laugh when he chatted with his women friends. His laughter was usually sardonic, mocking whatever emotions the moment demanded. It was sometimes dark and sultry. And it was always enticing.

He gave the mocking version now. "It's Bainbridge, after my father's youngest brother who died in Vietnam."

Gareth Bainbridge Clelland. She thought of the sleeping baby. William Bainbridge Gardenas. It sounded important, like somebody who was somebody. She nodded decisively. Yes.

"I need your keys," he told her. "I'll see if I can get the ute unstuck and down to the house this morning."

"We could call a tow service," she began, then remembered they had no telephone. She sighed in helpless anger with herself for getting into this predicament and involving her boss in it, too. He probably *would* fire her when they got out of this mess. "In my purse. I'll get them for you."

"Finish eating. There's no hurry." He glanced out the window nearest the table. "In this snow, nothing is going to happen very fast, I'm afraid."

Was he telling her they were trapped there until someone came to dig them out and restore the phone line? She'd already deduced that for herself.

She ate the meal, then excused herself. She rinsed and stored her dishes in the dishwasher, then headed for the bedroom again. Billy was still sleeping.

Moving quietly, she dug the keys out of her purse, carried them downstairs and laid them on the table. Gareth's dishes were gone and he was nowhere in sight. The doors to the rooms off the hallway were closed, so she couldn't tell which one he was using.

She hurried back upstairs, feeling as if she were intruding on his private domain, although no place could be more private than the master bedroom where she and Billy were staying.

Going through the French door, she crossed the sunroom to stand before the panels of glass. Although triple glazed, she could still feel the cold seeping in from the outside. The temperature was below zero.

Too cold to snow. That's what her grandad on the ranch in Wyoming used to say when she was little. However, he was wrong. It was snowing now, big, lazy flakes that tumbled from the sky as if carelessly tossed out the window of some celestial mansion.

The world was white, a wonderland of powdered sugar icing on mint chocolate trees. She wished they could stay here forever.

It was a startling thought. She went into the master suite and closed the French door behind her, putting aside fantasies for the warm comfort of her boss's bed.

She smiled. Shirl would faint when she told her about this unbelievable weekend.

Gareth exchanged his old corduroy shirt for a heavy wool one in red-and-green plaid, his jeans for old bib overalls that had been supplanted by new ones for skiing. He pulled on a pair of insulated boots and a wool hat. With a waterproof jacket, he figured he'd be warm enough to face the elements.

Grabbing the keys off the table, he went out the kitchen door into the garage. There, he fired up the old pickup he used in the mountains. It had a snowplow blade on the front. Usually he would have left the task until he was ready to leave, but he needed to check on Stacy's ute and the telephone pole.

He began a methodical pattern of pushing the snow off the drive. It was slow work and, at the rate the snow was falling, would have to be done again within twenty-four hours.

The morning passed before he reached the end of the drive and saw the ute in the shallow ditch.

Some invisible force grabbed his heart and squeezed it without mercy. He winced at the sudden pain, then cursed until it disappeared. Stacy and the kid seemed okay, so there was no use getting maudlin about what could have happened.

After scraping the snow away from the ute's path, he attached a chain to it, then hooked it to his rear bumper. It took thirty minutes of digging and packing sand under the wheels to get it free.

His breath formed dense clouds of steam in front of his face as he leaned against the side of the ute and wiped his face with a dry handkerchief. The thought entered his head that maybe he wasn't getting any younger. He gave a cynical snort. He was thirty-nine, but it had been years since he'd felt young.

He climbed in and cranked the engine of the ute. It started immediately. Easing it into gear, he pulled around the pickup and drove it down the lane to the house. He parked it in the garage. Inspecting the side, he noted the damage was minimal.

After hanging the keys on a hook beside the kitchen door, he lingered on the threshold. Something was different. He tilted his head to one side and listened intently.

The house was quiet, but it was always silent when he was in residence unless he turned the television on. No, the lack of noise wasn't what made it feel different to him.

It was something else, something more elusive, but alluring, like a melody carried on the breeze, making a mortal wonder if the sound had been the wind through the trees or the fluted notes of a fairy dance—

The rush of water in the upstairs bathroom made him realize what the difference was. The house wasn't empty anymore.

He pulled off his snow boots and padded across the kitchen in his socks. Upstairs, he paused at the open door and peered inside. Stacy was still in the bathroom.

Drawn by forces he couldn't define, he went to the bed and looked at the sleeping infant. Billy had had a bath and looked fresh and contented. Gareth noted the baby's hair was thick and black. He wondered if the father's hair had been the same.

Stacy's hair was dark, too, of a shade that was neither black nor brown. It had no blond or red highlights, only a glossy shine that spoke of health and cleanliness.

While he watched, the baby puckered its lips and made a sucking motion. Billy searched around with his hands and tried to find his mouth. When he couldn't, his tiny face screwed up, ready to cry.

Without thinking, Gareth reached down to help. The baby grabbed his finger and brought it to his mouth. Billy sucked noisily.

Gareth didn't move. Unnamed emotions churned, filling his chest and choking off his breath. For a stunned moment, he couldn't think.

Then the pain descended, the terrible pain of love and loss that was like no other he'd ever experienced, a pain he hadn't felt since Ginny's death.

He reeled from it, jerking his finger from the infant's grasp as if from a firebrand and taking a stumbling step back from the bed. He whirled and rushed from the room, not stopping until he was in the kitchen. He pulled his boots on and headed down the drive, walking fast... almost running... but for the moment there was no escape from the pain of remembering... the pain of loving....

Stacy opened the bathroom door cautiously. She thought she'd heard footsteps. She glanced around. The room was empty.

Probably Gareth doing something downstairs. Maybe he was preparing lunch. It was after one and she was starved.

After checking the baby, she went down to the kitchen. No one there. She wondered what to do. Going to one of the closed doors off the hall, she knocked gently. No answer.

"Gareth?"

When she got no response, she went to the next door, then the last one. Still no answer to her taps.

Unable to contain her curiosity, she furtively opened the bedroom door and peered inside. She started in surprise and opened the door wider. There was nothing inside.

The room was devoid of furniture.

She couldn't say why that startled her so. She retraced her steps and paused outside the door to one of the other bedrooms. Bolder now, she opened it. And felt the hair lift on her neck.

It, too, was empty.

The room was attractively proportioned. It was painted a very pale peach with white woodwork. A fireplace outlined with ceramic tiles, handpainted with wildflowers, took up most of one wall. Bookcases and cupboards formed an interesting and useful corner grouping to the right of it.

She imagined it as a sitting room, warm and cozy during cold winter nights. A family could read, watch television or simply gaze into the fire while the snow fell outside, which it was still doing at that moment.

Where was Gareth?

Going to the window, she saw a lone figure through the trees, facing into the wind, his head down, his arms pumping as he walked fast along the lane. He must be going to see about her ute. She'd heard the sound of an engine earlier and seen him from the upstairs windows as he plowed the driveway.

She closed the door and went to the one room she hadn't peered into. Opening the door without knocking, she again was startled by what she found. This room, too, had no furniture.

On the floor next to the inside wall, he'd unrolled a sleeping bag and added a pillow and blanket for his bed.

She pressed her fingertips to her mouth, distressed at the sight. The makeshift bed, the empty rooms... they cried out to her, speaking of emptiness... loneliness.

Tears welled in her eyes, blurring the outlines of the sleeping bag and silent room. She closed the door and leaned her head against it. The black despair she'd felt after Bill's death washed over her, only this time it was for her stern-faced, rarely smiling boss.

Taking a deep breath, she forced aside the despair, feeling utterly foolish for being so emotionally unstable.

She walked down the hall and stood in the middle of the living room. She let her gaze drift from feature to feature.

The room was comfortably, but expensively furnished. The sofa and love seat were of leather in a deep teal green. An antique desk was littered with his legal papers. Shining brass lamps and candlesticks gleamed in the snow-filtered light of early afternoon.

She returned to the kitchen with its eat-in table, the two sinks and multiple work areas, the double ovens, the separate microwave oven area. This was a house made for a family.

But Gareth had no family—no wife or children to fill the house with laughter and the clutter of hobbies and homework.

The tears erupted, and she covered her face with her hands and cried for him, for things she couldn't put a name to, for the pain of living, of loving, for dreams that couldn't be.

When she heard a vehicle in the drive, she fled up the stairs, grateful for its isolation from the rest of the house.

She washed her face and blew her nose while she regained her composure. Feeling better, she returned to the kitchen.

A woman's hormone changes after birth could lead to unpredictable emotional upheavals. That's what had caused the inexplicable tears. Gareth Clelland needed her sympathy like a leopard needed another spot.

She checked the contents of the refrigerator with an eye to lunch. Finding sliced roast beef and cheese, she prepared grilled sandwiches. While they were browning in the skillet, she rooted through the cabinets and came up with baked chips and salsa to add to the fare.

When she heard the motor of the garage door opener, she figured her boss was on the way inside. She placed the food on plates and carried them to the table. The door opened. She looked up and smiled. "Lunch," she announced. "Would you like beer or soda with your sandwich?"

His gaze ran over her, from the top of her head, over his robe that she wore, down to her shoes. "Beer."

She hurried to get it while he took off his snow boots and outer clothing. She brought it and a glass of milk to the table and took her place there.

"If you're bashful, you'd better keep your head turned," he told her.

She immediately looked his way to see what he was talking about. He had his bib overalls unsnapped and was in the process of sliding them down over his lean hips. He wore long underwear.

"My grandfather wore long johns in the winter. I've seen them before."

He shrugged and kicked off the denim garment. She got a glimpse of lean, muscled thighs and buttocks covered by pale blue waffle-knit cotton before he pulled on jeans and snapped them at the waist. He zipped them before he went to the sink and washed his hands, then splashed water over his face. He used a paper towel to dry with before coming to the table.

"I didn't expect a meal," he said, joining her.

"I was hungry when I woke up." She took a bite of sandwich when he did.

It felt odd to be eating across the table from a man again. She'd missed the companionship.

"Your ute is in the garage," he told her after taking a long swallow of beer.

"You got it out of the ditch?"

"Yeah. I thought I'd go back this afternoon and see if I could do anything about the telephone lines. The pole is okay. You didn't knock it over when the ute hit it, so maybe the line was jarred loose. I can probably fix it."

"Oh, good. I've felt terribly guilty for that. It was stupid of me to deliver the papers—"

"It was my fault," he broke in, his voice dropping to a deep growl. "I should have remembered the holiday and known everyone would be getting ready to leave town."

She nodded. "I wanted to get out, too. A drive seemed the very thing. If it hadn't been for the snow..." She trailed off, remembering it was more than snow that had detained her. "Well, anyway, I'm really sorry."

He waved her apology away with a sweep of his hand as if shooing a fly out of the way.

"I...uh..." She stared at the chip in her hand and wondered how to broach the subject. "I saw the sleeping bag," she blurted. "I thought you were sleeping in a bed." She couldn't keep the accusatory tone out of her voice.

He chewed and swallowed before speaking, his eyes on her all the while, making her feel uneasy, like the snoop that she was. She'd had no right looking into his empty rooms.

"I'm comfortable." He glanced outside. "The snow has let up. I'll be going out as soon as I finish lunch." He took a drink, cutting off further conversation while he finished.

Stacy ate more slowly. When he got up, she didn't say anything. He took the overalls and went into the bedroom he was using. He changed in there. When he came out, he put on his snow boots again. "I'll be gone a couple of hours. If the plow has been through the main road, I'll go down to the store and bring back some milk. Anything else you need?"

She could have named a bagful of items. "Diapers. A toothbrush. A bottle of hydrogen peroxide. Uh, how are your T-shirts holding out?"

"I've got plenty here, and there's a washing machine, so feel free to use all you need. They're in the third drawer down in the bureau."

She nodded her thanks.

"Anything else?"

"There is one item," she said, then wished she hadn't. She could make do until she got home.

He waited.

"It's personal."

"Okay." He was beginning to look a bit impatient.

"For women only." If she could only vanish on the spot.

He frowned, then relaxed as a comprehending gleam leapt into his eyes. "Okay, I get the idea." He left the room, obviously having no problem with female personal items.

A feeling like jealousy darted through her. She shook her head, perplexed by her own emotions of late. Naturally, the female body was no mystery to a man of Gareth's cosmopolitan experience and life-style.

In a minute, she heard his truck start up. The sound faded when he drove off. She finished lunch and put the dishes away.

Going to the master bedroom, she looked out the window for a while. She read, talked to Billy when he was awake, then took a long nap. When the baby woke her up, it was late afternoon. She sat in the rocker-recliner and put him to her breast.

At the first touch of his mouth, a strange sensation washed over her. Her breasts swelled, hard and painful, then, like a dam bursting, something gave way. A warm, pale liquid spurted from them, soaking her bra on one side, showering her son's face on the other.

He waved his arms excitedly and latched on, not having to suck at all as the milk flowed into his mouth. When the rush slowed, he seemed to have the knack of it. He suckled greedily, feeding until his tummy was taut and her breast was soft.

Laying him against her shoulder, she patted his back until he gave a loud burp, surprising her and making her laugh.

She lifted him to the other breast. After raising the footrest, she drew her knees up and laid the baby against them, then simply looked at him, amazed that this tiny creature was hers and proud that she'd had a part in his creation.

Her heart was awash with love for him, so full she felt she couldn't contain all of it inside her.

When Billy was finished and had burped again, she continued to hold him, marveling at this miracle of life.

"I love you," she told him, feeling fierce and tender at the same time. She smiled and wondered if all new mothers felt this way. "You're the handsomest, smartest baby in the whole world. Yes, you are, and I love you, love you, love you," she murmured in a singsong voice.

When she bent to plant kisses on his forehead, he grabbed her hair with both hands as it swung forward and held on.

"Ouch. What a grip," she exclaimed fussing to free the locks.

Straightening, she saw Gareth standing in the doorway, watching them. The expression on his face kept her silent.

He was staring at her and the baby, but his thoughts roamed far away, fastened on some image that only he could see. She didn't know what memories he recalled, but she knew a tortured soul when she saw one.

She realized Gareth Clelland was capable of deep feeling, not only capable, but that he had once loved someone to the depths of his being . . . and that he had lost that love . . . and never gotten over the loss.

He spun around and left without a word.

Chapter Four

Saturday dawned, so clear and bright, Stacy needed her sunglasses to look out the window. Light glittered everywhere, bouncing off the snow-encrusted rocks and trees and meadows, making her squint. The world literally sparkled.

She showered and dressed in her wool slacks and blouse, then tucked washcloths in her bra to catch the overflow of milk that came at odd moments. Every time Billy gave a cry, her breasts seemed to think this was a signal to produce.

"I should go into the dairy business," she told him when he ate later that morning. She sat in the rocker-recliner and observed a redbird checking a pine cone for nuts.

An outside door opened. She didn't hear it, but from upstairs, she felt the swirl of air through the snug house.

Gareth must be back.

For no reason, her heart bumped around her chest like a frightened thing. Which was ridiculous. She wasn't afraid of her boss, and she'd gotten over her embarrassment regarding his help during the crisis soon enough. There were only so many times a person blushed over the same event.

In a few minutes, she heard his muted footsteps on the stairs. He was probably in his socks. She'd noticed he usually left his boots in the kitchen. Whoever had housebroken this tough hombre had been brave.

She couldn't see herself suggesting he remove his muddy shoes before tracking through the rest of the house. Her husband hadn't liked being reminded of little things like that....

It came to her that she was comparing Bill to Gareth and that Bill was coming out the loser. She tried to recall the things she'd loved about her young husband when they'd first met, such as his quick smiles and laughter, but that seemed long ago.

Gareth appeared at the door. He studied her and her son for a long minute before he spoke. "The roads will be clear in another hour. The snowplows are out now. The telephone is working. You can check in with your doctor."

"Oh, that's a good idea." She lifted Billy to her shoulder and patted his back. He fussed at being removed from his lunch.

"If it's safe for you to travel, I'll drive you home this afternoon. There's a break between storms, but more snow is expected Monday."

"I'm sure it's okay. We're both fine, and I really need to get home." Having one set of clothing and no personal items was darned inconvenient. Gareth hadn't been able to get to the store yesterday and making do was getting difficult.

He nodded and left.

When Billy finished and fell asleep, she laid him in the cradle and went to the phone. She called Dr. Kate, reached the answering service and left her name, the telephone number and a brief explanation of her circumstances.

The doctor called back in ten minutes. "Are you trying to beat me out of my fee?" she demanded. "What's the idea of going off to the woods and having the baby behind my back?"

"I didn't plan it, I assure you." Stacy told her doctor what had happened, detailing Gareth's part with generous praise.

"Tell him I'm going to complain to the AMA. Practicing medicine without a license is a serious offense." She clearly thought the whole episode was hilarious. "Sounds like you had an easy time. How large is the baby?"

After Dr. Kate decided Stacy and the baby were in good shape, she told her she could go home at any time and to come in and see her on Tuesday morning. "Eight o'clock Tuesday. I'll come in early so you won't have to wait."

After they hung up, Stacy hesitated then called Shirl. She got the answering machine and left a message. "Come have supper with me tomorrow night and admire my big boy," she invited. That would blow Shirl's mind.

She went downstairs to find Gareth and tell him she was ready to leave. He was sitting at the kitchen table, his hands cupped around a steaming mug of coffee, gazing out the window.

"I can go home any time." She offered him a sympathetic smile for putting up with her. "I wondered if I could borrow the cradle to take Billy home in. I'll bring it to the office next week—"

"You can keep it," he said, his voice dropping into that deep growl that sounded dangerous but alluring at the same time. "For good," he added.

"Oh, but it's so lovely. You might need it when you marry and have children," she protested.

He smiled, surprising her with the bitter irony in it. "Do you think that likely?"

Marriage or having children? She didn't know which one he meant. One thing she knew—if he didn't marry, it would be by choice, not because of no willing partners.

She glanced at his boots next to the kitchen door. Some woman would be lucky. He was too sensuous a man to live life alone. The thought shocked her.

But really, her no-nonsense, rarely smiling boss was a man of unexpected talents and depths. She'd admired him from the first. She'd learned to like and respect him during the course of her job. Now she found herself evaluating him as something more than those character traits. She saw him as a man, one with a great deal of passion and tenderness to share . . .

Pulling her gaze from the boots, she met his eyes. He watched her with a serious, rather intense expression. Again she was held in a spell by that penetrating, lucid perusal.

He was the one who broke it. "Coffee?" he asked, rising and going to the coffeemaker next to the stove.

"Yes, please."

"I thought I would drive you home in your ute and spend the night at my place in town. I'll have a friend run me back out here in the morning."

Poor man. He couldn't wait to get rid of her. "I can drive. Dr. Kate said it was okay as long as I didn't feel weak or faint. Truthfully, I've never felt better."

"You look—" He stopped as if suddenly realizing what he was saying.

She wanted him to finish that statement. "Terrible," she supplied and laughed shakily. "I don't have any makeup except lipstick with me."

"You don't need it." He brought a cup of coffee to the table for her. "I'll fix lunch before we go."

He was determined to see her home. She didn't argue. Although she felt fine, she was nervous at being alone with a new baby. She was tired, and it was a long drive.

She thought of the night ahead. What if she went to sleep and didn't hear him crying? What if he choked?

She sat opposite Gareth and sipped the hot brew while worry darted through her.

"What's wrong?" he asked, frowning at her.

"I..." It seemed silly to voice her fears. "New mother syndrome, I think."

He nodded. "You're worried about taking care of him, that you won't be adequate."

She stared at him in amazement. "How did you know?"

"I once knew someone who had the same worries." For a second, his eyes flickered with some emotion she couldn't name, but it seemed soul deep.

Who had he known that intimately? But she didn't ask.

He moved toward the refrigerator. "My sister was like that, but by the time the baby was a couple of weeks old, she didn't think anyone but her, or maybe her husband, knew enough to take care of her daughter."

He was lying. She knew he was deliberately directing her thoughts elsewhere. There had been a woman one time, one that he'd loved. Maybe the woman had been married to someone else. His best friend perhaps. Gareth had fallen hopelessly in love with her. But of course he'd never reveal it by so much as a smile or a look of longing....

Fantasy. Pure fantasy.

She knew nothing about him. Besides, she had enough troubles of her own without taking on her boss's tragic past, if he'd even had one. Which she doubted.

"Well, I'll be glad when I feel like an expert. Maybe by the time he's twenty-one..." She let the thought trail away.

Gareth chuckled. "Yeah. If you can get them past drugs, alcohol and teenage pregnancy, you can feel proud."

"Amen," she agreed.

They ate soup, from a can this time, and sandwiches. She cleaned up the kitchen while he brought the baby, cradle and all, downstairs. His face was curiously impassive as he glanced at the sleeping infant.

He drove the ute while she watched the scenery go by and kept a protective hand on the cradle strapped onto the seat between them. She couldn't believe it had only been two days since she'd driven out so blithely, thinking to enjoy a ride before going home to an empty apartment.

That seemed ages ago. She was a different person now.

She glanced at the baby, then at the man who competently handled the ute, his mind miles away from there. He drove with both hands on the wheel, relaxed but alert. She would willingly place her life in those hands.

Sighing with the strange emotions that ran through her, she looked away and planned the rest of the weekend. She had to get groceries, baby items, a thousand things.

At the apartment, Gareth parked in her space in the underground garage at her direction, then carried the cradle while they rode the elevator to her apartment.

When they stepped off, her neighbors, a new couple in the building, stared at them in surprise. She spoke but didn't linger in the hall to talk. She was tired and drained all at once. Tears threatened. Her emotions were in a turmoil.

Hormones, she diagnosed and held on to her poise grimly. There was so much to do. And only her to do it.

Now she was feeling sorry for herself.

After unlocking and opening the door, she stood aside so he could enter and set the cradle down.

He looked a question at her.

"By the sofa. Set the cradle there." She forced a smile. "Thanks so much for your help. I can't tell you..." She trailed off, not sure what to say. Words weren't enough to convey her gratitude for his patience and kindness to her.

He placed the cradle carefully on the floor by the sofa. When Billy gave a whimper, Gareth started the cradle to rocking. The baby quieted at once. He straightened and came to the door, where she still stood.

Impulsively, she rose to her tiptoes and kissed his cheek, actually the lower edge of his jaw. That was as high as she could reach. She stepped back. "Thank you," she whispered.

He put a hand to the spot and rubbed it slowly. His eyes seemed to darken with mysterious thoughts while he stared at her as if she were a stranger.

"Do you want to call a cab?" she asked.

"No. I'll walk. It isn't far."

The door clicked shut behind him. Stacy sighed shakily. She couldn't figure out why, but she felt very much alone.

"He's beautiful," Shirl crooned, sitting on the floor beside the cradle and setting it gently into motion. "I want to take him home with me."

"Yeah? Wait until two o'clock in the morning when he's woken you up for the third time in two hours and tell me that." Stacy stretched and yawned wearily.

The previous night had been tiring. Billy didn't seem to know this was his real home and that being at Gareth's place had been an accident on their part. He'd been fretful most of the night, not sleeping for a long period until this afternoon. Stacy couldn't seem to regain her energy, but continued to feel tired.

"Being a godmother is like being a grandmother. We get to give them back when things go wrong." Shirl looked at her watch. "I've got to go. My latest heartthrob is supposed to call when he gets in tonight."

"I thought you'd sworn off traveling men after the last one," Stacy reminded her friend with a grin. "An airline pilot isn't exactly home every night."

"As soon as I saw him, I was smitten." Shirl stood and gathered her purse and jacket. She shook her head. Her gold hoop earrings swung wildly to and fro. "I can't believe the Great Stone Face actually delivered a baby."

"What else could he do? Throw me out in the snow?" Stacy smoothed her top down over her now flat tummy. "Why do you think a bachelor would have a handmade cradle at his hideaway?"

"It was probably there when he bought the place." Shirl studied her. "Hey," she said softly, "you aren't going off the deep end over him because of this, are you?"

"Of course not." Stacy was indignant at the idea. "But he was wonderful with me and the baby. So very gentle." She felt the heat rise to her cheeks at her friend's incredulous stare.

"'Cause if you are, let me tell you, I know a hard-shell case when I see one. No woman is going to reach his heart." Shirl paid no attention to Stacy's denial as she warmed to her subject. "I've watched him in action for three years. He never dates one woman exclusively. Never. And if one of them shows signs of wanting more, he cuts her out of his life ruthlessly." Shirl shuddered. "Hardhearted is his middle name."

Stacy smiled. "Maybe it's Beauregard," she suggested, then stopped. That was their private joke, hers and his. She didn't want to share it, not even with her best friend. "Actually, it's Bainbridge. I'm going to name Billy for him. William Bainbridge Gardenas. What do you think?"

Shirl stuck her hands on her hips and studied Stacy. A knowing look came into her eyes. "Girl, you got it bad."

Stacy shook her head, denying her friend's conclusion. "He isn't like you think. Just because Gareth is..." She searched for the word. "...Serious and rather stern-faced at the office, doesn't mean he can't have a sense of humor as well, or that he can't be kind."

"Bad, girl, bad." Shirl pulled her sheepskin jacket closed and zipped it. She'd been to a dude ranch for vacation last year and was now into boots and Western clothes.

Stacy grinned and gave up. Once Shirl got a notion, it stayed until rooted out by the next great idea.

"I gotta go. See you...when? Are you coming to work next week?" Shirl stopped by the door.

"I don't know. I'll have to check with the day-care center."

"Okay. Call if you don't show up."

After her friend left, Stacy went to her desk and looked over the list she'd made earlier. She'd planned on another month's salary before she took a brief maternity leave.

She wanted to stay home with the baby, especially now that she was nursing. Since that was impossible, she'd have to make other plans. First thing Tuesday, she'd call the nursery and see how soon they would take Billy.

"It's really terrible," Shirl confided in a low voice over the telephone. She was at her desk. "Absolute chaos. Janine quit in tears when Gareth snarled at her about a

mistake in a contract. 'Course she'd already gotten it
wrong three times before he told her, in that deadly calm,
deadly cold voice he uses with us lesser mortals, that his
year-old niece could do better. Janine threw the papers
down and walked out.''

Stacy groaned, picturing the scene. As executive assistant, she supervised the four clerk-typists in the law firm,
acting as a shield between the boss and them. Gareth did
tend to be rather abrupt. In adjusting to her son and
motherhood during the past month, she'd almost forgotten the office existed.

"Pete and Gareth had a shouting match last night after
everyone had gone but me. They were close to blows,''
Shirl continued, whispering.

Stacy assumed Gareth was in his office.

"I was looking for something to hit Gareth with when
he stalked out. Slammed the door after him, too. I'd never
seen him do that before. I rushed in to check on Pete. He
told me he was worried. He said Gareth had been acting
strange for days. He'd never seen the man explode like
that, and he's known him since their college days.''

"What were they arguing about?'' Stacy thought this
was strange behavior, too. Gareth, while serious, was always a gentleman. She'd never heard him raise his voice.

"Who knows?'' There was a tense pause. "When are
you coming back? It had better be soon. Before someone
gets killed.''

Stacy ignored the hyperbole. "I don't know. The day-
care center won't take a baby until he weighs at least ten
pounds. With Billy coming early, he's only a little over
six.''

Shirl sighed. "Gareth is going to be in court all next
week. With him out of the office, maybe things will calm
down.''

"Yeah, maybe." Stacy knew how he got when a case was in court. If he needed documents, he expected her to find them and get them to him immediately. With that frosted-steel voice, he could instill fear in the stoutest heart.

She and her friend talked a while longer, then made plans for Shirl to have dinner with her on Friday night. The new love would be out of town, flying a charter plane to Mexico.

After hanging up, Stacy finished folding the tiny clothes she'd washed that morning. The washing machine, which she and her husband had bought secondhand six years ago had conked out. The charge for repairs had been too much.

She'd reluctantly ordered a new one after several trips to the coin laundry. Those had been hell, juggling a baby and all the paraphernalia he required in addition to the clothes.

Not to mention the cost. Those machines gulped down money like there was no tomorrow. She figured she could pay for a new washer in less than a year at the rates they charged.

However, the new machine had taken a bite out of her emergency fund. That made her nervous.

She couldn't afford to take another month off, which was how long Dr. Kate said it would probably take Billy to gain the ten pounds he needed. The law firm gave a generous maternity leave, but it was without pay once a person used up her sick days, and Stacy, having been there only a year, had used hers the first week. Now what?

What if she took the baby with her to work?

Tingles danced along her nerves at the idea. Some offices let women bring their babies in while they were small. Until the children were big enough to crawl around, they shouldn't be a nuisance. Unless they cried a lot.

Billy was a good baby, sweet-tempered and usually content.

What was she thinking of? Gareth would have her head on a platter if she dared broach the subject. But it would solve a lot of problems.

If things at the office were as tense as Shirl indicated, she was definitely needed. And with Gareth in court all day...

The case would be a long one—patent infringement by a rival company against Gareth's client. It could take weeks. Or months. Certainly long enough for Billy to gain four pounds.

It was a crazy idea. But it would let her continue to nurse the baby for a few more weeks....

She tried to take a nap, but her brain kept buzzing with possibilities. Really, the baby wouldn't be a bother at all. She wondered who she was trying to convince—her boss or herself.

"Good morning. Clelland and Davidson," Stacy said into the receiver. She slit an envelope open with an efficient motion, checked its contents and laid it in the To Be Filed tray.

"Stacy?" a surprised baritone inquired.

She clutched the telephone as her heart zoomed up to mach speed. "Yes. Hello, Gareth."

"What are you doing at the office?" The surprise had disappeared and been replaced with a heavy dose of wariness, maybe even hostility.

She decided to tell the truth. "Shirl called me Friday and said Janine had quit and things were hectic. I thought I'd better come in and see what was going on."

A longish pause followed her explanation before he spoke. "Did your doctor okay it?"

"Of course. I had such an easy delivery, I could have come back to work the next week. Unfortunately the nursery school doesn't take babies that weigh less than ten pounds."

She shut up before she gave away the fact that Billy still didn't weigh ten pounds, and at the moment he was snoozing in the cradle under her desk. She pressed a hand against her midriff. As usual when she was nervous, her stomach felt as if she'd swallowed a boulder.

"Yes, well, I need a report," he said, ignoring her chatter about babies.

She wrote down the information and promised to send it by courier or cab at once.

"Or you can always bring it yourself," he suggested dryly.

It took a second for her to realize he was joking. "I only deliver during blizzards," she quipped, then realized that statement could be taken more than one way.

Heat crept into her cheeks as she recalled Gareth's aid in delivering the baby. It had been such a strange weekend, full of nuances and flickers of intense emotion and thoughts that remained unspoken between them.

"Same here." He chuckled, a rich, warm sound that dipped right down inside of her and dissolved the hardness in her tummy.

In sharing the birth of her child, they had shared something primal and instinctive, a thing usually reserved to the parents of the child. And she'd learned her stern-faced boss had a sense of humor. And a gentleness so sweet, she grew misty-eyed each time she thought of it.

"Will you be in the office this afternoon?" she asked.

"Not until late. I'm having dinner with the client, then I'll come by and check the mail. Leave me a memo of anything you think I need to do."

She was relieved. She'd be long gone with the baby before he showed up. "Right. I'm opening the mail now." She eyed the stack of letters. It was still three inches high.

"We got a little behind with it."

"I noticed." She didn't dare mention the problem wouldn't exist if he hadn't been so hard on the staff.

"You may as well say it—it's my fault Janine quit."

"Well, if the shoe fits..."

"A size twelve mistake," he admitted. "See if you can talk her around, will you?"

"Yes."

When they finished, she hung up the phone and pondered their conversation. Other than a couple of awkward platitudes and insurance questions they'd hardly spoken since he'd dropped her at her place a month ago. She couldn't believe she'd been brave or foolish enough to tease him, and he'd let her get away with it.

At a whimper from the kneehole of the desk, she bent and pulled the cradle out. She locked the door to her office, opened her blouse, then picked up her hungry son.

If her boss could see her now...

One week down. Stacy sighed in relief as she straightened her desk Friday evening. Gareth and she had corresponded by note and telephone during the day. He came in early and left for court before she arrived. He didn't get back until late.

So far, so good.

However, good luck only lasted so long. She'd checked with the nursery school earlier that day. They'd agreed to take Billy when he was six weeks old, no matter what his weight. If she could keep him hidden one more week, all would be well.

"Hi, fellow, how's it going?" Talking nonsense to him, she settled into her chair to let him nurse before she joined the throng of Friday shoppers at the grocery.

The feel of her milk coming down no longer caused her breasts to ache, although it still felt a bit odd. Each time she stepped into the shower, milk shot out in little streamlets for the first few seconds.

Dr. Kate had been delighted that she was nursing. "It's good for the baby and it's good for the mom," she'd informed Stacy while she checked her and Billy over. "It helps the body get back in shape faster."

Stacy had eased into her regular exercise routine two weeks ago without mishap. She'd never felt better. After a midnight feeding, Billy slept until six, so she was getting enough rest, too. Motherhood agreed with her.

Each time she thought of leaving the baby at the nursery, she experienced a pang of worry. As Gareth had predicted, she felt she was the only person qualified to take care of her son.

After burping Billy, she changed him to the other side, then rocked gently and hummed while she waited for him to finish.

A noise from the outer office caused the skin to prickle on her arms. Probably the janitorial service. She knew Shirl had locked the doors when she left.

The light clicked on in Gareth's office. She stared aghast as it spilled through the narrow crack of the partially open door into her office. She hadn't realized she hadn't closed it all the way when she was last in there.

She looked down at her son. His rosebud mouth worked busily, then stopped as he dozed off. If she removed him before he was finished, he'd let her know of his displeasure. Gareth would hear his squall easily.

Her mind spun haphazardly from one solution to another. She could say she'd picked him up from the nursery, then remembered something at the office she needed to do. Or that Billy had a runny nose and the nursery wouldn't let her leave him.

Footsteps crossed the adjoining room, sounding closer. Oh, no, he was coming into her office!

Her arms tightened around the baby. His head lolled to one side as he relaxed and fell deeper into sleep. She considered hiding under the desk until the office was clear.

But what if Gareth stayed until midnight or later going over his mail and catching up on office work? Maybe she should—

That was the way he found her, sitting on the edge of her chair in panic and indecision.

"What the hell?" His eyes, gray and stormy, narrowed as he took in the sight of her with the baby.

Their eyes met. For a split second, emotion flared in those cool, gray depths. She saw hunger and knew it was more than desire, but didn't know how she knew. She saw pain, then it was gone. His eyes moved downward over her. The hunger became pure, raw desire as he stared at her body.

She followed his gaze. Her breast was visible, a drop of milk clinging to the dark pink nipple.

Embarrassment swept over her in a torrid wave of heat. She adjusted her bra and pulled her blouse into place as fast as her trembling hand would allow.

"I can explain," she offered, dismayed to hear her voice quaver like a school kid caught in some mischief.

"Please do," he invited, emotion and desire swept cleanly from his face as if they'd never been.

She prayed for a softening of his icy expression, for any sign of understanding from him as she gave a concise explanation of her problem.

"Why didn't you stay home until the nursery would take him?" he questioned her as if they were in a courtroom and she a hostile witness. "I told you to take off as long as you needed. Surely you knew the job would be waiting."

"Things were chaotic here," she defended her actions.

"I should fire Shirl for calling you." He looked big and mean and menacing.

She worried he might do it. "It was my decision. I needed the money," she added, hating to admit anything that sounded like a human weakness to someone who obviously had none.

Her words seemed to jolt him. An emotion, too brief to be read, crossed his strong, angry features. "Why didn't you say so? I'll have the accountant cut a check for the time off—"

"No!" She returned his glare. "I'll earn my pay or do without."

"You'll stay at home another month and accept a salary," he ordered. "This isn't a damned nursery school. You can come back when your son is big enough to stay there."

"I can't accept a salary for nothing." Her pride was at stake. She wouldn't accept charity from him if she had to starve. "Besides, I don't see why I can't continue. This week has been fine. Billy isn't any problem in the office at all. He sleeps most of the time. I—"

He took two long strides forward. He loomed over her and the sleeping child. "Go home. I don't want to see you or your child here again. Is that clear?"

The blood drained from her face. "Perfectly clear."

He'd fired her. She couldn't believe it. She'd never been fired from any job. Not ever.

He stared at her another moment, then walked out. His office door closed with a jar behind him.

She sat there, stunned. Fired. A wave of fear washed over her. Her hands trembled as she slipped the shawl-like carrier around her shoulders and placed her son in it, snug against her body. He moved his lips, then settled deeper into sleep.

After gathering her purse and personal belongings, she glanced around the office to see if she'd missed anything. The plants she'd brought in could stay. She'd ask Shirl to water them until Gareth hired someone.

Fired. The word itself was a disgrace, yet she didn't think she'd done so very wrong. When she took a step, her toe hit the cradle. She stared at it for a long minute.

The cradle provided a key to his mixed reactions during the delivery, but she didn't know what secrets it hid. The cradle, his anger upon seeing her with the baby—all clues that pointed to something traumatic from his past. Had he and someone he loved had a child? If so, what had happened to them?

It was a mystery, one he'd never explain.

She removed the pad and baby blanket from the cradle and placed it on the floor in front of his office door on her way to the elevator. He'd find it there and take it to his place.

In a daze, she drove home, parked the ute in her space, then, still gripping the steering wheel, laid her head on her hands and let her mind drift.

She'd felt this way before. When her father had died, she'd felt the loneliness as a vast plain stretching before her. It had been the same when her husband had been killed.

As if sensing her distress, the baby awoke and cried. She pushed aside her worries. "This isn't the end of the world," she told him. "We'll be fine."

That felt like a terrible lie.

Chapter Five

Gareth paced the wall of windows in the penthouse that was his town residence. He stopped and glared at the cradle, then paced some more.

Get a grip, he advised himself. He'd hurt Stacy's feelings for no reason. No *good reason*. He had to apologize.

He closed his eyes and pressed a finger and thumb to the bridge of his nose. A steam engine chugged inside his skull, sending a shaft of pain through his head with each stroke.

Going into the kitchen, he found some aspirin and downed two tablets with a glass of juice. He refilled his coffee cup and leaned against the counter, wondering if Stacy was up yet.

Probably. Babies woke early as a rule.

A fresh pain lanced through his head. He couldn't figure it out. He'd seen other women with babies. They hadn't bothered him. But seeing Stacy with her child caused something to happen inside him, something painful that he didn't want, hadn't asked for and wasn't about to acknowledge.

That emotion-driven weekend at the cabin had started this internal battle. Before that, his life had been perfect. Well, not perfect, but certainly okay.

He paced into the living room. The sun was full up, spilling its warm radiance over the world. The cherry trees shimmered with new growth and ripening buds. Soon they would burst open. He realized it was the first day of spring.

There was no getting around his conscience. He had to apologize to Stacy for his hateful words yesterday. He grabbed up the car keys and the cradle that had silently accused him of unspeakable brutality all weekend and headed out the door.

There was little traffic this early on Saturday morning. He made it to Stacy's apartment complex in twenty minutes. In the elevator, he rehearsed what he wanted to say.

When the doors slid open, he stepped off, nodding to the couple who stared at him and the cradle in his hands. They got on the elevator. The man pushed the button. They stood there frowning at him until the door closed and hid them from view.

Going down the hall, Gareth realized they were the same people who'd seen him arrive with Stacy and her son the previous month. He'd been carrying the cradle then, too.

They probably thought the child was his. Did they also think he had refused to marry the mother?

A picture of Stacy leapt into his mind, her dark hair spread over his pillow, her courage greater than her fear as she told him what to do during the birth. Another facet of that odd weekend—he'd wanted her.

He'd looked at her in his bed and desire had poured over him like a flow of hot lava. Even in those moments of strain, when a contraction had her in its grasp, she'd looked beautiful to him, beautiful and desirable, the epitome of womanhood.

The trouble was, he'd still felt that way after the crisis had passed. When he'd walked into the office Friday and found her nursing the child, all the burning need he'd suppressed had gushed forth. He'd wanted to lie with her, not necessarily to make love, although that was part of it, but to hold her and the baby and...and what? Claim them? Keep them?

Some basic instinct had been awakened in him. He didn't know how to put it back to sleep.

Unidentified emotions churned in him when he stopped outside her door. He picked one out of the whirlpool—guilt. Stacy and her child were alone in the world, and he'd been an ogre to her about the baby. He'd make it up to her.

He rang the bell and heard it echoing in the entranceway on the other side of the door. He'd about decided she wasn't going to answer when he heard the click of the lock.

When she opened the door, he realized she'd been standing on the other side, observing him through the peephole and making up her mind whether to let him in.

"You forgot this," he said, his apology going right out of his head. He took in her appearance from the crown of shining hair gathered behind her head with a bow, down the loose top, past her slacks to the pink toenails visible beneath them. She was barefooted and looked like a girl.

Except he knew in the most elemental way that she was a woman and a very desirable one.

That fact frustrated the hell out of him. He didn't need to get involved with a transplanted wildflower from Wyoming. He wasn't going to get involved with anyone, period. He had nothing to offer a woman, not since...

"It belongs to you." She didn't open the door and invite him in.

"Got any coffee?" he asked, forcing the issue. "I'm not going to eat crow out here in the hall."

A startled expression flicked across her face. She stepped back and let him in.

After the door closed behind him, Gareth motioned for her to lead the way. She went into the kitchen. He placed the cradle on the living room floor where she'd had him set it the last time and followed her into the other room.

"I like your place," he commented, taking a seat at the table. Double windows faced south. A macrame frame with glass shelves had been suspended from the ceiling in front of them. Pots of herbs and flowers covered the shelves, adding a splash of color to the white walls and whitewashed pine cabinets.

The floor was beige linoleum with irregular dots of green and yellow, blue and red sprinkled in it. Stacy's home was clean and well kept, yet comfortable.

"Why are you here?" she asked. She brought him a cup of coffee and took her place across the table.

"To apologize for my behavior yesterday."

He watched to see how she would take his statement. She didn't blink an eye. Hmm, still angry with him.

"I hope you'll be speaking to me by Monday, or else it's going to be darned awkward carrying on a conversation through Pete or Shirl." He smiled at her.

She didn't smile back. "I won't be at work Monday."

A pang, sort of like alarm, went through him. "Why not?"

"You fired me." She gestured to the paper on the table. "I'm looking for another position."

"The hell you are." He forced himself to set the cup down without slamming it against the wood. "I didn't fire you. Why would I fire the best assistant I've ever had?"

"For having Billy at the office." She returned his glare with stoic courage. Her hand trembled as she lifted her cup and took a sip. "You said you didn't want to see either of us again. I took you at your word."

"I said that?" He racked his brain. He couldn't remember what he'd said, but he did recall his reaction at seeing her breast, full of milk, with a drop lingering on its tip. He'd wanted to catch the drop on his finger and taste it. He'd wanted to taste her.

"Yes," she said coolly, "you did."

He forced his gaze away from the front of her shirt and looked her in the eye. She was not going to let it go easily. "I'm sorry. I didn't mean it. I was . . . surprised at seeing you and the boy there, that was all."

She gave him such a skeptical look, he felt the heat rise in his ears.

"Surprised must be the understatement of the year," she murmured. She broke eye contact and gazed out the window.

"I'll expect you at the office Monday," he said firmly.

"I won't be in. The nursery won't take Billy yet."

"Bring him with you." He couldn't believe he'd said that.

Her eyes widened to their fullest.

He managed a grin. "Yeah, it shocks me, too, but I think it'll work. You can keep the baby at the office as long as you want. Until he gets to moving around."

"You mean it?"

"Yeah."

"But you hate children."

He glared at her. "Of course I don't. It's just that you caught me at a bad moment."

How could he explain what he didn't understand himself? Seeing her hold her child in love and tenderness opened a void inside him that he didn't want exposed. "You and the baby, you make me remember things I'd rather forget."

"Oh, Gareth, I'm so sorry."

Her voice, her impulsive kindness made him wonder just how far she would go to comfort him. And how far he'd let her.

When she made another murmur of sympathy, he felt it flow inside, warm and soft and healing. He'd liked her voice from the moment he'd heard it. While she had no discernible accent, there was a lilt to it, as if she'd been humming to herself before she spoke and the notes carried over into her words.

"It was years ago."

"But it still hurts." A pensive shadow crossed her face. "Sometimes it never goes completely away, does it? There's still the regret for all the things that could have been and guilt for those that did happen and shouldn't have."

It was startling to hear her voice the inner doubts that tore at him at odd, undefended moments. "Yeah, guilt," he echoed in the soft silence that followed.

"We have to learn to let it go, too. That's part of the process of grieving—letting all the useless stuff go."

"Have you?" He couldn't keep the cynical disbelief from the question.

"I think so. Having Billy helped a lot. There's an empty space inside, but it's a quiet place now."

"It doesn't hurt anymore?"

"Not unbearably."

He sipped the coffee and let the conversation settle in the back of his mind. The emptiness that haunted him receded until it, too, was bearable. He breathed deeply, slowly.

The peaceful tick of the clock filled the room with a busy cheer. Peace. Yeah, that's part of what he felt around Stacy.

"You have a soothing presence," he told her. "I noticed it at the first interview."

She looked pleased. "Is that why you hired me?"

"No. You had the brains for the job. Your references were glowing. Your old employer threatened me if I didn't treat you right. He said his son was a hired killer."

She laughed. "His son is a policeman. He worked with my husband for a time on the street. I was thrilled to get to work for you after Mr. Anders retired. He said you were one of the best trial lawyers he'd ever seen."

"So you'll stay on?"

"If you wish."

The tension melted out of him. "I do." His stomach rumbled. He hadn't eaten breakfast.

"How about some pancakes?" she asked.

He hesitated, knowing he should leave. But he wanted to stay. "Yeah, that sounds good."

They talked about world news while she prepared the meal.

The women he knew didn't cook. They hired a catering service. That was one thing he liked about his cabin in the woods. He prepared his own food. Simple meals for a simple soul, he'd once told his mother when she'd been horrified to discover there was no delivery service in a hundred miles.

Stacy glanced at him. "What are you smiling about?"

"Life."

"Care to explain that?" She brought a plate to the table and placed it in front of him. After setting out a pitcher of warm syrup, she returned to the stove. He noticed the smooth line of her hips in the snug slacks.

"When I was a kid, Sunday mornings were a big treat. My folks usually had some of their arty friends over for a brunch. Everyone would gather in the kitchen and talk and help with the meal. I'd forgotten how much I enjoyed those mornings."

"So there are good things to remember?" She gave him one of her encouraging smiles.

"Yes. Good things." He thought of the past, of being at the farm with Ginny, who'd found his mother's bossy ways and nosy questions somewhat intrusive. An understatement. "My mother thinks babies are the greatest. She'd probably bombard you with advice on raising yours."

"Does she know that you delivered Billy?"

He realized Stacy was still embarrassed by that. He wasn't, but he was irritated by the restless nights he'd experienced since the event and the recurring dream of coming home and finding Stacy in his bed again. Except in the dream her arms were open, inviting him in....

Stacy gave him a curious glance. He hadn't answered her question. "No, but I mentioned that you'd had a boy."

He waited for the pain of the past to strike with its memory of loss and emptiness, but there were other memories now...of Stacy holding on to him as she labored through a contraction...of her son, grabbing his finger, wanting nourishment from him....

Stacy left him alone and let him think about the past. That's what the police counselor had told her, remember the good things, let the rest go. She had, but having the baby had helped a lot. Gareth hadn't had that comfort.

She resumed reading the morning paper while they ate the meal. What a relief to know she didn't have to look for another job. She really liked what she was doing.

After a while, she looked up. Gareth was watching her. In his eyes was the hunger she'd thought she'd seen before. Now she didn't have to wonder if it was really there or not. It was.

"Gareth," she said, a protest. Or an entreaty? She'd sounded breathless.

He blinked, and it was gone. "Yes?"

She gazed at him in confusion. Didn't he know? "Nothing. It's nothing."

Restless, she turned on the radio, needing to fill the silence between them. Beautiful, haunting music filled the room. It fitted her mood, the restlessness inside her, the longing for things she couldn't name.

She stood by the window, letting her gaze roam the street and the tiny park across the way. Since the blizzard, the weather had turned warm, each day filled with sunshine as if apologizing for the earlier harshness. She closed her eyes and forced the moodiness at bay.

When she finally faced Gareth, she was surprised to see a look of intense sadness on his face. "Gareth?"

He gave a half smile. "Beethoven, isn't it?"

She nodded. "The *Moonlight Sonata*. It's one of my favorites." She didn't mention that its gentleness, then its passion called to her soul, making her want more than this meager existence. She longed for something...

Laying the paper aside, he stood abruptly as if suddenly deciding to leave. Instead he came over and stood beside her at the window. "I once knew someone else who loved it, too."

Her heart knocked against her ribs. He was sharing a tiny bit of his past with her. She instinctively knew he'd loved the woman who'd loved this music. Had she loved him? What had happened to her?

Stacy didn't dare ask.

The next thing that happened utterly surprised her. He lifted a lock of her hair and rubbed it between his thumb and finger. "She was a lot like you—warm and loving and—"

She was disappointed when he stopped, cutting the words off as if realizing he was saying too much. She stared at him. He was no more than a foot away. One step and they'd touch.

The heat from his body caressed her. She drew a shaky breath, let it out. It blended into the music.

He dropped the strand of hair and touched the corner of her mouth. She held very still. He explored her bottom lip with his fingertip. The sensation, as light as the flicker of an eyelash, sent currents of electricity into her chest.

Unable to get enough air, she had to breathe through her mouth. He outlined her upper lip, then removed his hand.

Slowly, so slowly she thought she would die before he reached her, he lowered his head. His lips touched hers, a glancing touch like a hummingbird skimming the flowers to find the very best nectar.

A thousand sensations ran through her, both sweet and painful, all demanding more.

"You'd better send me away," he murmured.

"No."

She slipped a hand behind his head and raised on tiptoe until she could reach his hard, unsmiling mouth. She gave him the same type of kiss he'd given her—an experimental touching that awakened the need for more.

Longing, visceral and urgent, spread through her. She moved closer, instinctively seeking the warmth of his large, hard body. Ah, he was like the sun, radiating heat that penetrated all the way through her.

"You make me feel warm," she whispered, kissing along his jaw, feeling the tension in the set of the muscles there and in his shoulders. She sensed the struggle inside him.

"You make me hot," he told her in a harsh tone. He clasped her by the shoulders, not letting her come closer.

His admission flew like a thunderbolt to some hidden part of her, shattering wisdom and common sense, filling her with unnamed yearning while music filled her soul.

"Do you know what you're doing?" he demanded, his voice going deeper, becoming husky with desire. It raged in his eyes, turning their coolness into heat.

"No."

The simple honesty of the word seemed to throw him for a loop. He stared down at her for a long moment. "If this happens, it's sex, nothing else. Is that clear?"

She tried to think, to will her body into submission, but it was impossible. Some part of her, strong and insistent, wanted to absorb the wonderful warmth his body gave off like a hearth on a cold morning. Another part wanted to give to him, to share a part of herself so the emptiness that caused him such pain could be filled and put to rest.

But these were shadows and flickers of emotions that darted through her mind, too swiftly gone to be captured and put into words. Somehow she knew this was the way, that right now he needed her touch as much as she needed his warmth.

"Is it clear to you?" she asked, wondering if he understood his own needs at all, or if he'd denied them so long, he could no longer recognize them. She leaned her head back so she could see his expression.

"Very."

He looked deeply into her eyes, probing to her very soul. Her heart beat rapidly, shaking her body while she waited, leaving the next move up to him. In that instant, she knew whatever was between them was much more than the desire of the moment, and that she'd waited for this all her life.

He moved his hands down her arms to her wrists, then to her waist and up her torso. He molded his hands over her breasts, measuring their size and fullness.

Stacy gave a little cry and pressed her face into his shirt. It had been so long since she'd experienced the spontaneous joy of passion, of letting herself feel the delight without fretting over the responsibility and worry that had gone with it.

"We're insane," he said. But he bent and kissed the side of her neck instead of letting her go.

And then his arms were around her. She locked hers around his shoulders and held on, shaking like a leaf in a gale. He held her closer. She felt every line and ridge of his body.

His lips found hers. This time the kiss wasn't a shy graze, but the full interplay of demand and answer. His tongue explored her mouth intimately. The kiss went on and on. An eternity of longing was exchanged. She knew the moment the kiss deepened and became more than a meeting of flesh.

Gareth felt her response as an explosion of fire and passion. With a soft moan, she twisted against him, merging planes and angles until they were melded into one. For a moment, he gave himself to it, to her, then with a wrench, he pulled his mouth from hers.

They stood locked together, their breaths loud in the silence and ragged with needs unmet.

"Gareth," she said.

Her voice stroked him as her tongue had, wringing floods of desire out of him like water out of a sponge. He couldn't bring himself to step away. He needed her like he needed air.

"No," he said. His voice made a mockery of the denial. It was filled with the husky cadences of pure, hot lust.

She smiled just a little. Her breasts, large and taut with nourishment for her child, rose and fell against him as she took a deep breath and let it out in a rush.

He took the necessary step to separate them. She let her hands trail down his chest, then drop to her sides. Her eyes, the barometer of her moods, showed disappointment.

That and the need to kiss her again had him clenching his hands in useless agony. He stuck them in the back pockets of his jeans and took another step back.

"I'm sorry," he said. The headache returned, a steam shovel digging through his brain looking for sense. It wouldn't find it. There was no sense in that ill-advised clench. And no future. "That shouldn't...I shouldn't have done that."

"It's because of what happened at the cabin," she said, her cheeks flushed, her hair disheveled from his caresses.

"Is it?"

He injected a note of sardonic amusement in his voice as a defense against feelings he didn't want to acknowledge. If they were going to be able to work together after this, he was going to have to find a method of communication that didn't include seeing or being near her.

"People who go through a crisis together often feel close afterward," she advised. Her seriousness—so damned sweet and earnest—mocked his cynicism.

He picked up his cup and took a drink, aware that she watched him, that she'd kissed him in the hollow of his throat and along his neck. Heat gathered deep inside.

"I've got to go." He set the cup down and stalked away.

She followed him to the door.

He faced her before he left, angry for reasons too complicated to explain, even to himself. "I should have known. It was there before. Your voice, your laughter, your joy at being pregnant . . . it was all there. You're real, and I want you."

"I feel the same."

"You're not supposed to agree with me." He felt fierce and close to exploding. He had to get out of there.

"Sorry ."

"The funny thing is I didn't know, not until this morning. During the birth, when you were in my bed, I was aware of desire, but it wasn't . . . real. Seeing you here . . ." He shook his head, not understanding any of it, then turned and walked out.

All the way home, he was haunted by her eyes, soft eyes that seemed to see inside his soul. He didn't like the feeling. It made him angry. He felt cornered, with nowhere to run to.

Worse, he hadn't wanted to run while he held her and she let him take all the kisses he could get. He'd been lost in the music and the frenzied beating of their hearts.

Desire—hot and sweet and urgent—rushed over him.

Gareth yawned tiredly as he settled deeper into a lounge chair on the patio. He hadn't slept worth a damn last night. Today was his mother's birthday, so he'd come out for lunch and to bring her a gold bracelet. She wore it now along with the diamond earrings his father had given her.

"There, what do you think?" she asked, adding a final dab of white to her painting. She sat back, then glanced at the two men in her life expectantly.

"Very interesting," her husband declared.

Gareth studied the picture. "I like the way the barn sort of teeters to one side. Looks as if it's on its last legs."

"Oh, does it?" She leaned close to examine her work.

His dad chuckled. "Perhaps if you'd use your glasses..." he offered as a suggestion.

"No." She straightened. "I tried those for a whole week. The world looked simply surreal, all stark lines and delineated colors. I like it better sort of misty."

"And no straight angles," Gareth added. He smiled when his mother wrinkled her nose at him.

She put her brush in turpentine and wiped the palette down. "How's Stacy and the baby?" she asked.

"Fine." As the pause lengthened, he added, "I don't see much of them. We're busy at the office."

"I spoke to Shirl Friday."

Gareth tensed.

"She mentioned the most extraordinary thing—that Stacy had the baby at your cabin during the blizzard."

Caught like a kid in mischief, he couldn't evade telling the story. He did so in as brief a manner as possible and made a mental note to tell Shirl to mind her own business.

"And you were snowed in for three days?"

He knew she wouldn't rest until she had the whole story. "From Thursday evening until Saturday morning. The snowplows were out by then." He provided a few more details.

"Well," she said and gave her husband a significant look.

"It was nothing," he insisted with proper modesty.

"I remember taking your mother to the hospital when you were born," his father said with a nostalgic smile. "It was during a concert to raise money for the symphony scholarship fund. She wouldn't leave until the intermission."

"You were very irritated over that, darling, but one can't walk out during a performance. It would be rude."

The two men looked at each other and burst into laughter.

She looked from one to the other. Her frown softened into an affectionate gaze. "I'm thinking of taking up archery," she announced suddenly. At their skeptical expressions, she explained, "Like one of those Greek deities ... what was the name?"

"Diana was the huntress," Gareth reminded her. "A virgin goddess," he added, tongue-in-cheek.

"No, no, not that one."

"Cupid was the other archer. He carried a bow and quiver of arrows," her husband put in.

She clapped her hands together in delight. "Well, there you have it," she said as if a puzzle had been solved.

A tingle of misgiving went through Gareth. He witnessed his parents' exchange of smiles that indicated a lifetime of sharing each other's thoughts. He flinched involuntarily as if an arrow had pierced his heart.

Or at least pinged off it, he added cynically.

His parents shared a wonderful relationship, and he was glad for them. He just didn't want any part of it.

A face appeared in his inner vision—Stacy, her smile encouraging as she told him to remember the good times and let the rest go. It wasn't that easy....

Then he remembered how easy it had been to slide his arms around her, to kiss her and take all the sweetness she offered in her kisses. He'd forgotten everything during those wild moments in her arms.

He sprang up from the chair, restless as emotion churned within him. He didn't like it. Passion ... love ... those were all part of the past. He didn't want to remember any of it.

"Are you leaving so soon?" his mother asked.

He realized he was standing in the middle of the patio, his fists clenched and ready for battle. He forced himself to relax.

"Yes. I have some papers to study before court tomorrow. Thanks for lunch." He kissed his mother's cheek and shook hands with his father before leaving.

On the drive back to the city, he realized his actions of late could be taken as *running*. From a woman and a kid? Ha.

Chapter Six

"I can't believe the Great Stone Face lets you bring Billy to the office." Shirl rolled her eyes.

Stacy rocked the cradle with her foot. Her son was sound asleep under her desk. He was such a good baby. "Billy weighs ten pounds now. I should put him in the day-care center."

"It's better for him to be with you. My mamma worked all my life, then she died. I never really knew her." Shirl collected the filing. "Take what you can while you can, is my advice."

"I could say the same to you. When are you going to meet the man of your dreams and marry and have children? By the way, how's your pilot?"

Shirl ran her fingers into her hair, which was in a frizz of bright tawny gold that was striking with her milk chocolate complexion. "I'm not seeing him." She pulled a long face. "I think there's something wrong with me. As soon as a man indicates he's really interested, I back off. He asked me to go visit his folks. Scared me to death.''

''When the right one comes along, you'll not give it a second thought,'' Stacy predicted, laughing at her friend's frown.

''Yeah, right.''

Stacy wasn't fooled by the flippant reply. Shirl was troubled. She knew the feeling.

Gareth was one of the most puzzling creatures she'd ever met. He'd finished the court case, winning it for his client after a tense, arduous trial. He'd been in the office during regular hours most of the week. They hardly spoke.

He dealt with her by phone, using the intercom rather than speaking directly with her as he used to. He kept the door between their offices closed.

Probably a wise course. It would give them both time to get over this madness. Of course there was the possibility they wouldn't. Then what?

''I've got to go.'' Shirl straightened and gave a yawn.

Stacy was tempted to tell her friend of Gareth's visit to the apartment, but she couldn't do it. It seemed much too private and intimate to share. Besides, she didn't want to hear Shirl's laughter when she confessed what had happened.

After her friend's departure, Stacy contemplated those passionate moments for the hundredth time. She touched her lips and remembered how his had felt against hers.

She couldn't fall in love with her boss. It wasn't done. It certainly wasn't wise. However, she had a sinking feeling that all the pep talks she'd tried for days weren't going to do a bit of good.

The ringing of the telephone halted the recriminations. ''Good morning. Clelland and Davidson.'' She tipped the cradle with her foot, rocking it in case the noise woke the baby.

"Hello. Stacy?" It was Gareth's mother.

"Yes. Good morning and how are you, Mrs. Clelland?"

"Frightful. Would you believe I've sprained my ankle? Can you believe this would happen when I'm expecting a hundred people here for an auction Sunday?"

"Oh, that's really too bad," Stacy murmured in sympathy.

"It's a disaster." Actually she sounded quite cheerful about it. "That's why I'm calling. I wanted to know if you could help out this weekend. I wouldn't ask, but I'm really quite desperate, and I don't know where to turn."

"This weekend?" Stacy repeated as she scrambled for something to say.

"The proceeds of the auction go to the local children's literacy program. We have some really nice items. Gareth talked one of his friends into donating an antique automobile. Isn't that exciting?"

"Uh, yes."

"So do say you'll spend the weekend and be my legs. I know it's crass of me to ask, but Gareth has mentioned how terribly efficient you are. Please say you can come."

"Well, I . . ." Stacy didn't know what to say.

"Is Gareth there?" his mother continued. "Let me speak to him. It would be best if you came out tomorrow."

Tomorrow was Friday. Stacy had been looking forward to the weekend as a relief from the tension in the office. She certainly didn't want to spend it at his mother's home.

"I'm really sorry, Mrs. Clelland, but I have a baby—"

"Yes, I know. Of course I expect you to bring him, too. Now, is my son there? Let me speak to him," she said without waiting for an answer.

"I'll get him." Stacy, feeling as if she'd been swirled around in a whirlwind and spit out, buzzed Gareth on the intercom. Five minutes later, he strolled into her office.

"How do you feel about spending a long weekend in the country?" he asked. "We'll go down tomorrow and return Monday."

Trying to read his expression was like studying a blank wall for a hidden message. "I don't know."

She realized she wanted to go. She'd like to meet his parents and see where he grew up. However, during the past two weeks, they'd regained much of their former equilibrium in working together. Perhaps it was best not to rock the boat.

"Don't be scared," he said on an ironic note. "I'll control my beastly impulses."

"I'm not scared." She spoke too fast. "I mean, of course I'm not scared. It's just that... the baby and all."

"He does okay here at the office. He'll be fine at the farm. There's a nursery. Mom will put you in the adjoining room so you'll be close." He hesitated. "She does need help."

He didn't like the idea of her being there, either. She considered the pros and cons of the situation and decided nothing could happen with his parents and a baby in attendance. "All right. If you think I would be useful."

"I can guarantee it. Mom will run you ragged. I'd advise comfortable clothes and shoes. Also, our guests will feel more at ease if the hostess is dressed casually."

She mulled over this last cryptic remark after he returned to his office. She wasn't a hostess. She was an employee.

Sometimes it was hard to remember that, especially when the memory of that passionate embrace invaded her mind and refused to be rooted out as it had so many times the past few days.

Gareth gave her a critical once-over while he stored her bags in the trunk of his sedan. He affixed the baby's seat in the rear of the car, facing backward. Stacy strapped her son in and tried not to look as apprehensive as she felt.

Soon they joined the other residents leaving the Washington, D.C., area for the weekend. The interstate highway traffic was already bumper to bumper.

"It might take a couple of hours to get to the farm," Gareth told her. "Usually I can make it in half that time."

"The traffic is heavier than I'd expected." She couldn't think of any idle chitchat and so sat in silence, watching the urban crowding thin out into rolling countryside. When it did, they were able to pick up speed.

Mansions were sometimes visible behind fences and hedgerows. She wondered what kind of house was on his parents' farm. Was it a real farm, or some rich person's idea of a farm—twenty acres with a swimming pool and a couple of horses to add color?

The air in the luxury vehicle hummed with undertones of tension, or maybe it was just her. She was going as an employee, not a guest, and certainly not as a friend or...or anything. There was no need to be excited about the trip.

When they turned into the drive that swept in a circle along the front of a massive two-story brick house, she stared at it in dismay. It was grander than anything she'd imagined.

"It looks...old," she said inanely.

"About 150 years. My grandparents bought it and spent most of their retirement years restoring it. My grandmother still sends interesting bits and pieces back from her travels. This drives my mom wild trying to find someplace to put all the junk, as she calls it. I think that's why she has the auction each year. So she can get rid of it.''

Stacy didn't say a word. She held Billy while Gareth retrieved their luggage from the car. A tall, thin man in a black suit rushed down the steps.

"Mr. Gareth, welcome home. Here, let me take those." He took over the luggage.

"Stacy, meet Jacob. He can answer any question or provide any reasonable service." He spoke to the older man. "Ms. Gardenas is here to help Mom with the auction this weekend. Would your niece be available to keep an eye on Billy for us?"

"She'll be delighted. Your mother has already arranged it."

They'd arranged a baby-sitter without consulting her. Stacy didn't want one. Billy would stay with her.

"Ms. Gardenas will want to interview Kim to be sure she's qualified to take care of a very young child. I believe she's had experience with babies, hasn't she?"

"Indeed she has. Her older sister has three children. Kim has helped raise them. Also, she's majoring in child psychology at the university."

"How's she doing?" Gareth asked. "She was having trouble with one professor last year, if I remember correctly."

"Straight A's this time. She made the president's list."

"Great." Gareth glanced at Stacy. "Ready?"

She nodded and followed him up the steps and into the house. Her heart thumped very loud as she entered.

The inside of the mansion was as she'd expected—marble and brass and crystal chandeliers, scroll-footed sofas and lyre-back chairs and piecrust tables. A maid in a black uniform.

"Your mother thought Ms. Gardenas would be comfortable in the nursery quarters." Jacob inclined his head toward a broad hallway, indicating she was to go first.

"I'll go find Mother and say hello," Gareth told her. "I'll be back for you in, say, a half hour?"

"Yes, that'll be fine." She hurried along the hall.

"Last door on the right," Jacob directed.

She opened the door and went in. Her breath caught. Done in pale green walls and white woodwork, with white furniture upholstered in a floral print with lots of green, the room looked like a garden.

Living plants lined a tiled area next to a window that started a foot from the floor and went almost to the ceiling. Yellow and white daisies in earth-toned ceramic pots decorated the three tables in the room. The four-poster bed was draped with gauzy white netting and swags to match the upholstery.

A door stood open at one side. Through it, she could see the nursery. A whitewashed pine crib and dressing table were aligned along one wall. A bureau sat in a corner. A rocking chair and table were next to a window that looked out on a sweeping lawn and swimming pool.

A barn was visible in the distance. A tractor, big and important-looking, was parked beside it. A horse grazed in the pasture next to the barn, and corn grew in the field beyond that.

A working farm. That made her feel more at ease.

"I'll send Maudie to hang your things," Jacob told her. With a smile, he left her.

She laid her purse on a table, then took Billy into the nursery and changed his diaper. He'd slept all the way here in the car, so he wouldn't need a nap before bedtime. She sat in the rocker and played patty-cake with him, then put him in the crib while she freshened up.

The maid she'd seen earlier knocked and entered at her call. "I'm Maudie. I'll hang your things. What do you want to wear for dinner? I'll unpack it first in case it needs pressing. The family usually gathers in the library between six and seven."

Since it was a working weekend, she'd brought office suits. "The black suit," she decided.

Maudie efficiently unpacked and hung her clothes. She surveyed the black suit, then selected a white silk blouse. "You won't need the jacket," she advised. "Did you bring a gold necklace and earrings? They would go well with the skirt and blouse. Ms. Clelland said you were to borrow whatever you needed from her."

Stacy lifted her chin. "I have my own things."

She wasn't about to borrow finery from Gareth's mother like a poor relative visiting from the sticks.

After changing into the other clothing, she cleaned her face and put on fresh makeup, using a bit more than she usually did. She hoped no one noticed her hands were trembly. If they had before-dinner drinks, she'd probably spill something all over herself. She grinned at her reflection.

She wasn't here to impress possible future in-laws. She was here to work. She'd keep that firmly in mind.

When Gareth knocked on her door at exactly six o'clock, her stomach went to her throat and remained there. She picked up her son and held him like a shield. "Come in," she called huskily.

Gareth opened the door. He, too, had changed and now wore dark slacks and a blue silk shirt that made his eyes resemble polished pieces from a summer sky.

"Won't you join us?" he asked formally.

She nodded. Billy grinned at Gareth and reached out a hand to him, surprising them both. She watched with suspended breath as Gareth put his finger in the child's hand and let Billy bring it to his mouth for a taste.

After an experimental nibble, Billy let go and waved his arms the way he did when he became excited. He wanted Gareth to hold him. Fortunately, her boss didn't get the message.

"Mother is dying to see the baby," he said. His gaze lifted from Billy to her. It lingered on her mouth. "She thinks I'm deliberately depriving her of one of her natural rights, that of being a grandmother."

Stacy's lips tingled with the memory of his mouth on hers. Sometimes that seemed more like a dream than reality. "Lots of mothers feel that way."

"Do you?" His smile was sardonic as usual when conversation turned to anything remotely personal.

"I might. When Billy grows up."

"Mother will also try a bit of matchmaking between us. Don't let it get to you." With that, he motioned for her to follow and led the way down the hall.

Staring at his broad back, too stunned for words, she felt a contraction in her chest. For a moment, the tiniest moment, she wished Gareth was Billy's father. And if he was Billy's father, then he would also be her husband....

His parents waited for them in the library or study or whatever they called it. Gareth made the introductions. "Stacy, the invalid, looking suitably wan and dramatic in black, is my mother. The gentleman in the smoking jacket is my father. He's the only person outside the movies I've ever seen wear one of those and get away with it."

Stacy quickly looked at his folks to see how they took his teasing. They were smiling easily.

"We're delighted you could come," Mrs. Clelland said.

Mr. Clelland stood and shook Stacy's hand. He escorted her to a chair next to his wife, who sat on a velvet chaise longue like a languid movie queen. Stacy kept expecting someone to shout, "Lights. Camera. Action."

"Oh, look at the little darling." Mrs. Clelland touched Billy's cheek. He grabbed her finger and sucked on it. She laughed as if this were a great feat. "He looks just like you at that age," she exclaimed, giving her son an oblique glance.

Gareth looked momentarily startled, then he laughed. "I suspect most babies look alike for the first few months."

"Not at all," his mother insisted. "Molly always wore that quiet, stubborn look from the day she was born. Our daughter out West," she explained to Stacy. "She married a rancher—he was a widower—and now has two children. He had a little girl by his first wife, and he and Molly have a daughter, too."

"How nice," Stacy said sincerely, again feeling caught in a whirlwind as Mrs. Clelland breezed through the family history.

"Our hopes are on Gareth for a grandson. Molly's husband says they aren't having any more children."

"What does Molly say?" Gareth slipped in with a wry twist.

Mrs. Clelland laughed and clapped her hands together "She says they are."

The noise scared the baby. He held his breath, then le it out in a cry.

"Oh, I've frightened the little one. Here, Billy, woul you come to me and let me comfort you? Come, let m hold you. It's been so long since I've held a baby." Mrs Clelland took the baby from Stacy and held him to her sill clad bosom.

Stacy worried that he would drool on the woman's elegant dress. "Here, you'll need this." She slipped a cloth diaper under Billy's chin on Mrs. Clelland's shoulder.

The conversation became general after that—a discussion of the weather and its effect on the farm. She discovered there was a farm manager who lived a quarter mile away and brought them fresh eggs and milk every morning.

"And we'll have lettuce from the garden with our dinner," Mrs. Clelland promised as if this were a rare treat.

Stacy ventured to ask about her duties while there.

"Mostly I need you to put number stickers on the rest of the items, then record the sales price beside the number on the master list," Mrs. Clelland explained.

Dinner was announced. Stacy retrieved Billy, who was trying to suck on Mrs. Clelland's pearl necklace.

"I took the liberty of having the bassinet brought down from the attic," her hostess explained while her husband tucked her into a wheelchair for the trip to the dining room.

"Did you now?" Gareth asked, grinning at his father.

"Yes, I did. Before I hurt my ankle. I'm not usually so helpless, you know." His mother waved him and his remarks aside and spoke to Stacy. "I thought I could help with Billy while you and Gareth finish the list of auction items."

"Of course." Stacy found the bassinet in the dining room, newly decked out in embroidered cotton frills, with a fitted sheet and blanket in blue with horses cavorting over them. "How lovely," she said softly, pleased at the thoughtfulness.

"I used it for both my children. It was so handy. See? It's on wheels so you can move it wherever you wish with no trouble. That's why the nursery is on the first level."

"How nice." That was all Stacy could think to say.

"Now about the auction," his mother continued when they were seated around an oval table of shining walnut. "You will be in charge. Gareth and the servants will do what you tell them."

Stacy darted a glance at her boss to see how he took this. A lazy smile appeared at the corners of his mouth. His voice, when he spoke, was vibrant with genuine amusement. "Mother thinks men were put on earth to do her bidding."

"Of course they were. Now, where was I?"

"Putting the sales price on the master list," Stacy reminded her. "Who takes the money?"

"Jacob or Maudie will do that. You'll collect and count it when the cash register gets full. You'll have mostly checks. Gareth will put everything in the safe for you."

"And what will Father be doing?" Gareth asked.

His mother gave him a lofty perusal. "Taking care of me. He'll push my wheelchair so I can mingle with our guests." She turned to Stacy. "There'll be a buffet at noon. The caterer will handle that. Check it once in a while to see that there's plenty." She paused and considered. "I think that's everything. If a question comes up, do whatever you think is best. I'm sure you won't have any problems."

Stacy wished she felt as confident. Mrs. Clelland seemed to think Stacy directed charity auctions as a matter of course in her spare time. She pointed out this was her first

"I will be available to advise you," Mrs. Clelland stated

While Mrs. Clelland beamed at her, Mr. Clelland gave her a sympathetic smile. She smiled back, instinctively liking the older man. He took his wife's bossiness with becoming deference to her wishes, which in no way seemed to diminish him as a man. He shared his son's intelligence and dry wit, but without using them as barriers around his heart.

The evening passed pleasantly, but by ten Stacy was getting tired to the point of wanting to be alone. They had returned to the library after the meal. Maudie had taken Billy to the nursery and tucked him into bed at Mrs. Clelland's request. Stacy yearned to go check on him.

At a break in the conversation, Gareth spoke up, "I think Stacy needs to retire now, Mother. She'd answered enough questions for one night. So have I."

"It's so delightful to have a baby in the house again," his mother told her warmly when she stood. "Tomorrow you must let me keep him. Would you mind?"

"Of course not."

"It was wonderful having our grandchildren here for Christmas. If Gareth would put his mind to it and do as well, his father and I would be so very happy."

Stacy couldn't suppress the flush that rose in her face at his mother's pointed look at her son. Gareth's soft laughter rang in her ears, mockingly amused.

He had warned her, but surely the woman wasn't really thinking of her as a mate for her son. Stacy sought his gaze, but he'd returned to looking out the window at the night sky.

She jumped into the conversation to break the escalating tension. "Christmas was made for children, wasn't it? I'm looking forward to Billy's first tree. If you will excuse me, I am rather tired."

She said good-night and started from the room. Gareth did the same and fell into step beside her. They walked down the broad oak-floored hall to the room adjoining the nursery.

"Don't let Mother run over you. Tell her to butt out when she oversteps your boundaries," he advised.

Stacy doubted Mrs. Clelland would listen to anything she said. The woman was a law unto herself, but very likable. "She's a lovely person. Bossy, yes, but kind, I think."

"Umm, yes. She likes people, but she tends to sweep them into her projects, then it's like fighting a whirlpool to get out. Sometimes it can't be done. My sister moved out West and I moved to the city to get away."

Stacy felt her neck grow warm as he described her feelings concerning his parent.

He chuckled, catching her discomfort. He slipped a hand behind her neck and rubbed the tension away at the base of her skull. "Don't worry. I'll stay close in case you get sucked in over your head."

She smiled as if grateful and slipped inside her room. With the door closed between them, she wondered who was going to save her from *him*.

In the bedroom, she quickly slipped out of her clothes and into a thick cotton nightgown that buttoned down the front. She sat in the rocker and nursed her son, her mind on the man she'd left in the hall.

A thousand questions about him haunted her. If she ever got a moment alone with his mother, would she dare ask about his past, assuming his mother would tell her anything?

He was such an internal person, she doubted he'd ever told anyone if he'd been in love. But surely he had. That house in the woods cried out for a family. And she hadn't imagined the emptiness. Yes, she'd ask if the opportunity came up.

After feeding Billy, she changed his diaper and tucked him into the crib. He grabbed the blanket with one hand and stuck his thumb in his mouth. He offered her a sweet smile, then closed his eyes and went to sleep. She thought he was the most beautiful baby in the world.

Going into her room, she looked through a magazine and read an article on raising a generous child rather than a selfish one. Finally she went to bed. Just before she fell asleep, her mind went off on a tangent of its own.

Thoughts of how good life might be if she was married to Gareth danced through her brain. For a while she let the fantasy play itself out, but reality intruded before she got to the part where he was holding her and kissing her breathless.

Frowning at the wayward musing, she put it firmly out of mind and drifted into sleep.

Saturday was an impossibly beautiful day. Stacy dressed in slacks and a pink blouse. Wearing comfortable sandals, she went to find her hostess. Maudie directed her to the patio on the shady side of the house.

Ms. Clelland was in the wheelchair, her leg propped up to ease the discomfort of her injured ankle. "Ah, there you are. I trust you slept well?"

"Yes, thank you." Actually she'd been restless, waking several times during the night for no reason. Each time she'd been aware of dreams centered around Gareth disturbing her sleep.

"The men are playing tennis. They'll join us for breakfast when they're through."

Stacy had already noticed Gareth's tall, powerful form on the court. His father played opposite him. What the older man lacked in brute strength, he made up for in strategy, running his son from side to side, trying to force an error.

"They're both very good," Stacy commented, tearing her gaze from Gareth with an effort.

"Yes." Mrs. Clelland studied her while Stacy poured a glass of orange juice and a cup of coffee from a tray on a sideboard.

Stacy felt rather flushed and wondered if Gareth's mother could see her reaction to the woman's handsome son. She took the glass and the cup to the table and sat opposite Mrs. Clelland.

"I think you would be good for my son."

Stacy wasn't sure she'd heard correctly. "I beg your pardon?"

"I've shocked you." Mrs. Clelland laughed merrily. "All mothers are matchmakers. Just wait until your little one grows up and starts noticing girls. You'll have definite opinions on the one he should choose."

Stacy tried to set the woman straight. "Gareth is my boss. There's certainly nothing...that is, we haven't...we don't..."

"Oh, I'm sure nothing has happened." Mrs. Clelland's tone was droll, her expression exasperated as she watched her son lob a tennis ball over his father's head. "Gareth is so circumspect, I sometimes wish he *would* do something illogical or illegal."

"He drove ten miles over the limit on the way down here," Stacy felt compelled to mention in his defense.

"Did he now?" Mrs. Clelland's eyes twinkled. "Would you pour me another cup of coffee?"

"Of course." Stacy refilled the cup, then returned to the table. The breeze lifted her hair away from her face, cooling the heat brought on by Mrs. Clelland's astute glance. It also carried the sounds of the men's conversation as they heckled each other or complimented a particularly good shot.

"It was three years ago last Christmas that Gareth's fiancée was killed," his mother said aloud as if musing on it to herself.

Stacy stared at her aghast.

"He was devastated. It was only a week before the wedding. They were expecting a child, a surprise because Ginny didn't think she could have children. Naturally, I was overjoyed. Neither of my children had married or given me grandchildren at the time."

"How did she die?"

"A car accident. The other driver had been drinking."

"How terrible." Stacy pressed a hand to her middle where pain lodged like a boulder ready to shatter.

That was the emptiness then—a fiancée, pregnant with their child. He'd never gotten over it. Her heart ached for him.

"Yes. Gareth retreated into himself. I was beginning to think no one could reach him. And then you came along." His mother smiled happily.

"Mrs. Clelland, I think you're seeing things that aren't there," she said as gently as she could.

"No. I saw the way he looked at you last night. He's aware of you as a woman."

"It's...you don't understand. He helped me when Billy was born. It made things seem different for a while, but not for long. It was a temporary madness."

"The first he's had since Ginny died."

"But he's dated other women. I've heard him on the phone with them."

"Dated, yes. He's a healthy male animal. With you, there's more. There's caring." She laughed softly. "I couldn't have planned anything better than your having the baby on his doorstep. It opened his eyes."

The conversation was getting out of hand. "Really," Stacy protested, "you're wrong..." Her voice trailed off. Gareth had told her he wanted her, and there had been those kisses....

"Marry my son," his mother admonished gently, watching the two men finish their game. "He needs you and your child. He needs to feel again, to trust life again. He needs to take a risk with his heart, but he's afraid."

Gareth afraid? Stacy didn't believe that.

Mrs. Clelland sighed. "You think I'm an interfering old witch. I probably am. But promise me you'll take anything he offers. My son is an honorable man. He'll take care of you. If you let him. I'm asking you to do so. His need is so great."

"I...I don't know what to say."

"Say yes." Mrs. Clelland gazed at her intently. "You're the one who can save him from the blackness that eats at him day after day. Make him laugh again, Stacy. Please."

"I...I'll try," Stacy heard herself promise. That wasn't much of a risk, to make him laugh. She hadn't agreed to seduce him or anything like that. She could imagine his anger if he'd overheard this strange conversation.

The moment might never have been. Mrs. Clelland was all charm and laughter when the men joined them at the table. It was so unreal, Stacy wasn't sure the conversation had taken place. Maybe it had been part of the fantasies her subconscious had been busily weaving around them for weeks now.

"How about a game before the slave driver puts us to work?" Gareth suggested after they ate.

"I'm too rusty. You would be bored."

"Do go," his mother encouraged. "Maudie will bring Billy out the minute he wakes up, so you mustn't worry about him."

That took care of her next line of argument. Feeling like a weed among the roses, Stacy changed to shorts and tennis shoes. She went to the tennis court and revived her college game.

"You're good," Gareth complimented when she placed a shot straight down the line, thus winning the point and the game.

Her gaze met his. For a minute, she was filled with pride because she could at least keep up with him. "You're going easy on me."

"A little," he admitted.

He won, but not by a terribly wide margin. Walking to the house, she realized she felt alive in every cell. When she peeked at him, he was watching her, a sexy, mysterious expression in the depths of his eyes. She looked away, flustered by the male interest.

"Were you always shy?" he asked. "Or is it just with me?"

"With you."

Maudie appeared with Billy. Stacy rushed to her son, glad for the distraction while she got her feet firmly on the ground once more. The conversation with his mother had sent her mind in directions it shouldn't go. When he looked at her as if she were beautiful, her imagination winged off on its own.

"Stay here," Mrs. Clelland invited when Stacy would have gone to her room. "Nursing is natural and done in the best circles today. Could I burp him for you?"

"You may as well give in," Gareth told her, "or else she'll hound you to death."

"Well, if you don't... if you think it's all right..."

He nodded. The two men spared her blushes by turning away from the table and talking about the corn crop in the field. She listened to their conversation while her son ate hungrily. She remembered her dad and grandfather talking about crops and ranch details in the same fashion.

A farm was a good place to grow up. Gareth had been happy here, she decided. He'd had a horse and lots of friends. His parents were somewhat eccentric, but they loved him.

He had loved a woman once, and she'd died.

Stacy observed his profile while he talked to his father. She recalled the bleakness in his eyes when his guard was down. Life was bleak when grief was your only companion. She knew. She'd lived through it.

It was foolish to think she could ever open that dark, empty place inside him and fill it with light. She wanted to, but only he could unlock the door and let another in.

However, she'd promised she would try to make him laugh. Perhaps that was the key. Lowering her gaze, she watched her son with grave tenderness. There were more ways than one to skin a cat, her grandfather used to say. Maybe there was more than one way into a stubborn man's heart.

Chapter Seven

Stacy began to understand the extent of Mrs. Clelland's maneuvering when it took her, Gareth, Jacob and the son of the farm manager all of three hours to finish the master list and tagging of the auction items. His mother could have directed the entire operation from her wheelchair.

By midafternoon, the task was done.

Stacy stood in the middle of the carriage house. Like the main house, it had been restored to pristine condition.

The scent of wax and lemon oil permeated the air. Every piece of furniture had been shined to a high gloss. She'd had Gareth and the men arrange the donated items like rooms in a home. Smaller items were displayed on tables and dresser tops as part of the domestic scene.

Outside, a buffet would be set up in a tent by the catering company first thing in the morning. Tables and chairs would go under the maple trees. Champagne, fruit punch, coffee and tea along with various snacks would be served all day.

"That's it," Gareth declared.

His grin was one of satisfaction. He looked incredibly handsome in a pair of cutoffs, tennis shoes and a blue cotton work shirt he hadn't bothered to button.

Sweat gleamed on his chest. A couple of drops glistened from the thick swirls of dark curly hair. The waistband of his shorts was damp with it.

She longed to run her hands over him, to taste the salty flavor of his skin, to kiss the grin from his face. She thought of a quiet corner in a barn loft, hidden by the bales of hay usually stored there.

"We'll ask your mother what she thinks," she said.

"She'll love it," he predicted.

She did. "Yes, this is perfect, Stacy. Perfect. You did a wonderful job." Mrs. Clelland beamed all around at her workers and thanked each one warmly. After Jacob and the young farmer left, she turned to Stacy and Gareth. "It's time for our guests to arrive. You'll want to shower and change."

"Uh, guests?" Stacy questioned on the way up the flagstone path to the house. She glanced at her beige slacks and pink blouse. Definitely grungy.

"A few in for dinner, a few for cocktails. Six couples will be spending the night." Mrs. Clelland waved her hand airily as if it were nothing to have twelve people overnight. For her, it apparently wasn't.

Stacy pressed a hand to her stomach. "I can eat in my room," she ventured. "Or the kitchen."

"Nonsense. I'll need you to help with the hostess duties. I can't get around very well, you know."

Gareth gave a snort of laughter. His eyes met Stacy's as he held the door open while his father pushed the wheelchair.

"Mother is about as helpless as a boa constrictor," he muttered for her ears only after the older couple was inside. "You've probably noticed."

Stacy tried to hold in a smile, but it was impossible with his eyes gazing into hers in silent laughter.

"Ah, yes, I see you have," he continued as if complimenting her on being astute.

She fled into the house before she laughed aloud. "I'll go change now. What time are we supposed to...uh..." She couldn't think of a polite word.

"Report in?" Gareth finished for her.

His mother checked the time. "It's almost three. Let's have drinks on the patio at five and watch the sunset before we have dinner. By the way, we'll dress tonight, but tomorrow will be casual." She beamed a smile at Stacy.

Stacy felt her heart sink. How formal did they dress for dinner? She smiled uneasily and headed for her room. She'd hardly gotten inside before there was a knock on the door. She opened it, expecting to find Maudie.

It was Gareth.

He came in and closed the door.

"Yes?" Impatience coated the word. She wanted to check on her son. Maudie had brought him to her for his afternoon feeding. Now he should be asleep.

"Go check on him," he said, reading her mind.

She hurried to the nursery and opened the door. Billy was asleep in the crib, a brown-and-white teddy bear, obviously new, tucked in with him.

Maudie was in a chair, reading a magazine. She looked up. "Hello. He was an angel, slept all afternoon," she assured Stacy, hopping up. "I'll go to the kitchen and help with dinner, if you don't need me anymore?"

"No, that's fine. Thank you, Maudie."

The woman smiled and left. Stacy peered over the railing at her son. He looked very contented. As usual, her heart melted.

"He's a fine boy," Gareth said quietly, coming to stand beside her. It was the first remark he'd made about the baby.

"Thank you," she whispered, her heart full. She turned her head and looked at him.

He motioned her from the nursery and followed when she left, closing the door silently behind them. They stood in the middle of her room, each watching the other. He took the two steps needed to bring them within an inch of touching.

He waited, his eyes on hers.

Unable to resist, she laid her hand on his chest, then raked her fingers through the matted curls. His skin was sweat-slicked and smooth under her caress. She detected the hardness of bone and muscle in his large frame. She sensed his strength.

He took her left hand and laid it beside the right one. To her surprise, he closed his eyes while she hesitantly explored his torso. She licked her lips, then bent her head forward until she could touch him with her tongue.

His breath caught, then released, but other than that, he didn't move. She moved her lips over him while her hand gripped his waist above the cutoffs. Finding his nipple, she tasted it with her tongue, then nibbled at it. It beaded into a tiny ball.

A tremor ran over his skin like a sudden chill, causing similar one to run over her.

She lifted her head and stared into his eyes.

They were dark, the pupils wide in the dim room, burning with needs he didn't, or couldn't, hide.

"Gareth?"

"Yes," he said. "To whatever you're asking."

He enclosed her in his arms, bending his more massive body over hers, fitting them together carefully, as if their lives depended on an exact blending of curve and angle.

"Put your legs around me."

She did. An electric shock ran through her at the intimate contact. She felt him through the cutoffs, hard and rigid and ready for her.

He moved two steps back and settled in a chair, her legs to either side of his. He rubbed her back, soothing and exciting her at the same time. His gaze never wavered from hers.

"You need to rest."

"No, I'm fine." She spoke quickly, breathlessly.

A hint of a smile touched the corners of his mouth. "I never thought I'd feel this way again. It's been murder all afternoon, watching you, listening to your voice...."

Currents raced up her back as his voice trailed off. He slipped his hands around her and cupped her breasts.

"Does this hurt?" he asked, kneading her gently.

"No. It...I like it."

"So do I." He hesitated. "May I taste?"

Her breasts swelled against her bra. "Yes."

He opened the pink blouse and pulled the material from the slacks. He studied the maternity bra, then opened the nursing placket. "Beautiful," he said in a deeper, softer tone.

A drop of pale liquid formed at the tip. He caught it on his finger and brought it to his mouth. Then he dipped his head and rubbed the hard tip with his tongue.

Sensation pelted down her chest, into her abdomen and lodged in a secret, welcoming place inside her. She held the back of his head with one hand and rubbed his shoulder with the other.

"I didn't come here for this," he muttered, drawing back and looking at his handiwork. "Do you have anything formal to wear tonight?" He palmed her breast and caressed it tenderly.

"I brought a crushed velvet skirt," she managed to whisper. "And a lace vest."

"Good. I want to taste you some more." He waited for her nod before opening the other side and laving her breast with his tongue. She arched her back instinctively.

His hands cupped her hips and guided her forward. Through the layers of material, she was aware of his desire as much as her own. She moved against him, eliciting a groan or a growl from him. She wasn't sure which. She wondered if they were going to make love.

Gareth is an honorable man.

His mother's words echoed through her skull. An honorable man. If he made love to her, would he feel compelled to marry her? What of her own honor? Would she want to force him into marriage against his will?

She knew the answer to that.

But for this moment, she could pretend. He'd go no further than she indicated she wanted to go. Somehow she knew he would know where that boundary was.

Cupping his head in her hands, tenderness warring with fierce desire, she urged his mouth to hers.

The kiss shattered her world into a kaleidoscope of whirling rainbows. They fought a lover's duel, the battle ground roaming from her mouth to his and back again.

He caressed her a thousand different ways, with a thousand different nuances of pressure, on her back, her shoulders, her breasts. She did the same.

When she pushed his shirt off his shoulders, he helped her, letting it fall to the floor. Then they were wrapped i each other, flesh to flesh, hands moving, exploring, restlessly seeking the other.

It was the most wonderful experience of her life. His hands cupped her bottom. He pressed her hard against him with a sudden, desperate motion. "Don't move," he whispered hoarsely, burying his face in her neck.

She sat utterly still, except for her hands in his hair. She stroked through the damp, silky strands as if to soothe him.

When he at last raised his head, it was to gaze into her eyes for a long time. She returned the look as steadily as she could. He brushed the wisps of hair off her forehead with hands that weren't quite steady.

"Sorry," he said in an odd tone.

"That's okay."

His smile mocked himself. "No, it isn't." He grimaced as if irritated with the uncontrollable passion. "Worse than a teenager. Thinking with my body instead of my brain."

"So was I," she admitted. The intimacy of their position was somewhat awkward. She tried subtly to disengage her body from his.

He slipped his hands to her waist and held her. "I think we need to talk." His glance went to his watch. "But there isn't time, not with a houseful of people due any minute. I came to tell you not to worry about clothes. My parents' friends will be in anything from jeans to vintage clothing to formals."

"Thank you for telling me. I wasn't sure..."

It struck her as an odd conversation to be having with her still sitting astride his lap, her breasts against his chest, her arms around his shoulders, his big, warm hands moving over her.

He must have had the same thought. "This is insane," he murmured, then he kissed her again, a soft, sweet kiss that made no demands on her.

For another minute, they indulged the embrace, then with a sigh on her part, they parted. He let her slide off him, then stood with one fluid motion. He crooked a finger and lifted her chin until he could see into her eyes.

"That was the most exciting experience I've had in years. Next time, I'll make sure it's the same for you."

She forced herself to hold his gaze. "I'll hold you to that." She tried to look sophisticated and cool about it.

His eyes darkened. For a minute, she thought he would carry her to bed and keep his promise right then. But he heaved a deep breath, grabbed his shirt and, after one last caress, left her.

She sank into the chair, unable to stand on her own for a few minutes. Doubts rushed over her. Did he love her? Or were his kisses the impulse of the moment?

Hearing a clock strike the hour, she realized time was running out. She went to shower and get ready for the evening.

"Stacy, how lovely you look," Mrs. Clelland complimented her when she arrived on the patio a few minutes after five. "Good, you brought the baby. Is he awake?"

"Yes." Stacy wheeled the bassinet to her hostess.

Gareth sat on the low brick wall surrounding the patio, a brandy snifter in his hand. He gave her a solemn perusal as if to see if she were all right after their tempestuous embrace. Mr. Clelland brought her a glass of fruit punch.

"Thank you."

"Isn't he precious?" Mrs. Clelland crooned. She looked from Stacy to her son, her eyes full of mischief. "You two would have lovely children."

Stacy nearly choked on the punch.

"Mother, you're embarrassing our guest," Gareth chided lightly. He turned to her. "You look lovely, by the way."

She glanced down at her skirt. The crushed velvet was deep amethyst. With it she wore a cream satin top with a lacy vest of the same color that reached almost to her knees. The vest was embroidered with jewel-toned flowers. She murmured her thanks and selected a chair close to the baby.

Something was wrong. She didn't know what it was, but she could feel it. Gareth had withdrawn into his office persona—polite but remote. The bleakness had returned to his eyes.

She wanted to protest, but what could she say? Don't remember the woman you loved? Don't remember she carried your child? It was impossible to say anything. He'd retreated to a place she couldn't reach.

"Our guests have started to arrive," Mrs. Clelland said. "They'll join us in a few minutes. I thought it would be nice to have some private time just for family."

Stacy glanced at Gareth to see how he took this blatant prod from his mother, but he was watching the clouds backlit by the sunset on the far horizon. Arriving at a decision, she rose and went to him.

He didn't look at her when she stopped beside him. She felt the barriers surrounding him like a barbed wire fence around a prison. She and the baby had brought his emotions to the surface. He was trying to force them into the void again. That wasn't the way to deal with the past.

She leaned against his shoulder, moving into his space and forcing him to acknowledge her.

When he looked up, she smiled at him. Although he returned it, sadness lay deep in his eyes along with other emotions too deep to read. Guilt, he'd told her when they'd listened to the music at her apartment. Guilt and regret and sadness.

A tough load to carry alone.

It was all a part of grief, and grief needed to be shared. She'd had him and Shirl when she'd needed help. Later the thought of the baby had brought her comfort. Gareth hadn't let himself need anyone.

The sound of other voices broke into her introspection. Two couples came in and were introduced. The other four arrived fast on their heels. Jacob lit the patio braziers when the air turned cool. Maudie served hot hors d'oeuvre while Mr. Clelland poured drinks for everyone.

Three of the couples were older friends of Gareth's parents. The other three were closer to Gareth's age, invited with him in mind. Stacy was acutely aware of the speculation in every pair of eyes as she was introduced.

"Stacy is helping me with the hostess duties," Mrs. Clelland explained in her breezy fashion. "She's been a lifesaver, taking over the auction for me on short notice. This is her son, Billy. He's a darling baby, isn't he?"

Eyes darted from the child to her, then to her left hand. She no longer wore a wedding ring.

"I'm the executive assistant from Gareth's office," she quickly explained before anyone got the wrong idea.

"Stacy keeps things humming on an even keel," Gareth put in. He laid a hand on her shoulder. "Even me."

There was general laughter from the group. Mrs. Clelland beamed in open pleasure. The other couples seemed to take it as a given that she and Gareth were a couple, too.

When Stacy turned a questioning gaze on him, he returned it with a steady look that spoke volumes...if she could only read his cryptic thoughts. He pressed her shoulder, then let go.

The talk became general after that. They went into dinner at last. She didn't know if it was because of nursing the baby, but she was hungry more often of late. Later they returned to the library for coffee.

The baby woke with a whimper.

Stacy went to the bassinet and lifted him. "I think I should take Billy to his room now. It's getting cool out here."

"I'll help," Gareth offered. He held the door open and pulled the bassinet inside after them.

He led the way to the nursery at the back of the house. They were silent on the trip down the long hallway. She tried to thank him at her door, but he entered with her.

The nursery quarters were lit only by a night-light. The atmosphere shimmered with dark intimacy. Gareth pushed the bassinet into the baby's room and left it by the wall where it would be out of the way.

"They think we're a couple," he said while she changed Billy's diaper. "Do you mind?"

She hesitated, then shrugged. "I'm not responsible for what they think."

His wry laughter, quickly gone, surprised her. "Mother is. She's forcing us together. I'm sure she thinks she's helping some great cosmic plan." Now it was he who hesitated. "It would be easier to play along, if you think you can take it."

"Play along?" She looked up, then went back to putting Billy in his pajamas.

"Yes. For us to be seen together will please her. It'll also keep the other women off my back."

She couldn't help but smile.

He grinned, too. "That sounded incredibly egotistical, but it's a fact. Women . . . come on to me."

Stacy laid the baby in the crib. "It's a thing to be expected if you're handsome, wealthy and intelligent."

In the silence that followed, she glanced around. Gareth wore an odd expression, almost as if he were stunned.

"Surely that doesn't surprise you," she said. She removed her lace vest and laid it over the end of the crib.

"Is that the way you see me?" His voice had a rich, quiet timbre that soaked right down to her toes.

"Yes." She paused with her hands at her blouse. "I've got to feed the baby. I'll have to take my blouse off to keep from wrinkling it."

"Do you want me to leave?"

She didn't know quite what to say. To be embarrassed after he'd touched her so intimately that afternoon seemed foolish. "I don't want you to think I'm coming on to you." She gave him a bold glance, then spoiled it by laughing at his chagrin.

"I won't think that. We need to talk anyway."

She laid her blouse aside, then lifted the baby and sat in the rocking chair. Billy suckled hungrily, his tiny hand holding her finger where she pressed her breast away from his nose.

"About this afternoon?" she asked. Oddly, she found she wasn't embarrassed by the passion they had shared. For those few moments, the bleakness had disappeared from his eyes.

"Yes."

Instead of talking, he turned the straight-backed chair they had sat in earlier and straddled it, his arms crossed over the back, and studied her while she fed her son.

"Your mother told me of your fiancée," she said at last. "Is that why seeing me with Billy makes you sad?"

"It makes me remember," was all he would admit.

"What was she like?"

His fists knotted and turned white at the knuckles. "Why do you want to know?"

"Grief is something that should be spent. If you store it inside like miser's gold, it will turn on you, becoming bitter and rancid. Talking about the good times can help. What did you and she like to do together?"

"Besides make love?" he asked harshly, his expression closed and angry.

She gazed at him steadily. He was hurting, and he wanted to hurt back. "All couples like to make love. What did you do afterward? What was her favorite date?"

He dropped his head and rested his chin on his hands. Ever so slowly his grip relaxed. He took a deep breath and started. "She liked music. I took her to concerts. Afterward... it was the best..."

"Yes, I know what you mean. Bill and I liked long drives and picnics in the country. Making love after a Sunday drive was the sweetest time of all. Once he got stung when we sat in a field of clover." She laughed softly at the memory.

"That must have put a crimp in his style." His laughter joined hers.

"Well, one does have to improvise at times." She put the sleepy baby on her shoulder and closed her bra. She patted his back until he burped, then turned him to the other side.

"That's incredibly beautiful," Gareth murmured. His eyes darkened to a moody intensity.

"Nursing the baby?"

"Yes. It's sexy, but something more...something tender and endearing ... I can't describe it."

"I think I know what you mean. Nursing is connected to life and being human and caring about someone else."

He frowned. "It can hurt . . . this caring. Or cause others to get hurt."

"Sometimes it can happen that way." She gave him a sympathetic glance. His face had closed, his expression turning inward. The anger had returned.

He stood and pushed the chair aside, then paced the room. "Save your pity. I don't want it. My life is fine the way it is. If you'll carry out our little pretense until this weekend is over, that will keep my mother off our backs."

"All right." She kept the disappointment out of her voice. For a minute, she'd thought they might break through the anger. Gareth had to get past that and accept what had happened before he could come to terms with it. "Why do you blame yourself for your fiancée's death?"

He stopped dead still. "It was my fault," he said without looking at her. "I called and asked her to pick me up at the airport. Because of me, she died."

"Because of a drunk driver," she corrected. "You weren't responsible for him."

"But I was for her. If I hadn't called, if I hadn't been so impatient, she wouldn't have been on the road at nearly midnight on Christmas Eve. I was selfish, thinking of *my* needs, *my* wants, not her safety."

"No one can control events—"

"You don't know. You don't know anything about it." He strode across the carpet. The door closed with a soft click behind him.

She thought of the steps of grief the counselor had told her about. First, disbelief, then resentment, guilt, anger and last of all, acceptance. Gareth was still locked in guilt and anger. Until he let those go, there was no room in his heart for another.

* * *

The nightmares were back.

Gareth watched the activities around him as if he were a being from another planet, invisible to the Earth creatures. He felt curiously cut off from them, untouched by their humanness.

Except for one person.

Hearing Stacy's laughter, he searched the crowd until he found her. She was talking to one of the men his mother had invited to the cocktail party last night. A TV producer of nature documentaries. Stacy found that fascinating.

Yeah, she liked handsome, wealthy, intelligent men. The producer scored high on all three.

He turned away, his mood as black as the night he'd shared with the crickets and owls. Unable to sleep, he'd walked for hours, until fatigue had forced him to bed.

Then the tangled, twisted dreams born of desperation and guilt had taken over.

They'd been all mixed up, one minute featuring Ginny, the next Stacy. And the baby. In slow motion, the cars had collided in his dreams all night. Like a photograph, the scene had become imprinted in his mind—one of wrecked metal and torn bodies, of blood and death and horror. Stacy and the baby had died . . .

The need to see the child forced him outside. Walking past the guests who milled in and out of the carriage house, he stopped on the lawn and shaded his eyes with his hand. Stacy had been nervous about leaving the child with a stranger until he'd suggested Kim bring Billy outside.

There, in the shade of an old maple tree, Jacob's niece read a book, the bassinet with the baby within arm's length. Nearby, the caterers were laying out the buffet in the huge white tent. Pennants flew from the corners and center post.

The tent reminded him of a picture he'd seen in a book about King Arthur and his knights. The scene struck him as unreal, with nothing in common with the world as he knew it.

A world of law and logic, that's where he was most at home, not the one of rioting emotions and tantalizing passions.

"Gareth, hello. Did you see what that snuff box went for? I was amazed." Stacy lowered her voice. "Your mother's friends must have tons of money."

She laughed, and his heart went into a spasm. He frowned, not liking the feeling.

"Well," she said, her smile fading. "I have to feed Billy now. Kim said he'd been an angel all morning. I want her to keep a good opinion of him."

She walked away. Everything in him wanted to call her back, to say something to make her laugh again. He clenched his fists. He didn't need this. He didn't want to feel anything for anyone.

A flood of memories washed over him. Recent memories. Yesterday, holding Stacy, touching her, tasting the sweetness of her breasts, those moments hounded him. They, too, had been mixed up in his dreams.

There was one confession he hadn't made when she'd insisted upon talking about the past. For three years he hadn't been able to make love to another woman. Not once. His body simply hadn't responded to another female. Yet with Stacy, he'd responded fully, like an adolescent in the first throes of unbridled lust.

When Stacy spoke to Kim, then took the baby and headed for the house, he followed at a safe distance. In the privacy of the back patio, she settled in a chair and took the child to her.

Unable to look away, he watched, like some perverted Peeping Tom, while she nourished her son. Strange sensations raced along his nerves, making every muscle ache with tension.

He wanted...he wanted...he didn't know what. Something more than the life he had now, something more than he deserved. He closed his eyes, but the image of Stacy and little Billy stayed as if burned into his eyelids. Beyond that was the image of fire and wreckage...of death.

The anger rose in him. Useless, stupid anger. Anger hadn't been able to put Ginny back together and make her whole and well. He'd wanted to kill the driver who'd run over her, but that wouldn't have brought her back, either.

He opened his eyes, forcing himself to face the harsh light of day as he had three years ago. It had been his call that had brought her out on the road that night. It had been his selfish need to see her that had killed her. That was the truth he had to live with night after night. That was what haunted his dreams and turned them into nightmares.

There was no use in thinking about it. He forced the memories into the void where nothing touched him. Glancing at the patio, he saw Stacy watching him with a troubled expression. He walked forward and sat on the wall near her.

"Things seem to be going well," she said with a tentative smile. "Your mother was pleased with the number of people who showed up for the auction."

"She's always pleased when there's a crowd."

The smile fled at his harsh tone.

"I'm sorry. I didn't mean to sound cynical. Actually, I like people, too—the more, the merrier."

"Because you don't have to confront yourself when you're in a crowd?" she asked, giving him an assessing once-over, her gaze as cool as a breeze off a glacier.

He felt her words like a blow. "Who appointed you my counselor?" he demanded, dredging up the anger, letting it take over before he confessed his soul to her and crawled into her arms like a child needing comfort.

"Do you need one?"

Too restless to sit, he paced the patio. "No." He met her gaze and turned away, unable to face the sadness and pity in those warm, velvety depths.

"Then you'll have to work through this on your own," she advised. "You'll have to forgive yourself and realize that you have very little influence over other people's actions—"

He whirled on her. "Dammit—"

The baby let out a wail, cutting off the angry words that gathered like a knot in his chest.

Stacy held Billy to her shoulder and patted his back. "There, now, there, darling. It's all right," she soothed him.

The need to lash out increased. Gareth sucked in the balmy April air and held it along with the angry words. He wanted to tell her she didn't know anything about how he felt or what he was thinking. She could take her two-bit psychobabble advice and stick it—

With an enraged shake of his head, he stemmed the hot tide that trembled on his tongue. Anger was no good, he reminded himself. He'd learned that three years ago. The emptiness was better. No need to feel or react to anything. No emotions, no mind-blowing passion. Yes, go for the black void.

He tried a smile. It was probably more of a grimace, but he managed it. His effort wasn't noticed. Stacy was busy with her son, laying him across her arm while she brought him to her left breast to nurse.

Gareth couldn't tear his gaze from the very feminine sight or the tenderness on her face that went with nurturing her child. It tore into him, opening the chasm, ripping at its edges until the pain became too much.

With a curse, he headed for the auction and the safety of the crowd. Funny, he'd never before thought of himself as a coward, but here he was, running from a woman and a child again.

Chapter Eight

"The servants are off today. We'll do our own breakfast," Mrs. Clelland explained to Stacy. "How did the little one sleep last night? Did you get enough rest?" She poured batter into a waffle iron and closed the lid, then checked the bacon and sausage browning in the oven, limping a bit as she moved about.

"Billy and I slept fine," Stacy said. Hers had been the sleep of exhaustion. Running the auction and seeing to the buffet had taken a lot of energy.

After she'd retired to her room, she'd sat by the window for a time, her emotions churning with needs she'd given up on fulfilling years ago. While sitting in the dark, she'd spotted Gareth outside on the broad sweep of driveway.

The loneliness of his solitary figure, out walking in the night, still haunted her. She wondered if she and the baby were part of his troubled thoughts as he roamed the darkness in search of peace. She thought they were.

They had breached a gap in him that he didn't want breached. Their presence opened an old wound that had never healed. Before helping her with the delivery, he'd lived in a world devoid of emotion. He wanted to hang on to that void.

He was strong-willed enough to do it.

While no one could go back to yesterday, a person could remain stuck in the past, guilt forever eating at the soul and destroying the possibility of another love.

That would be a shame. Gareth was that rare man with the depth and steadfastness a marriage needed, who was also able to inspire the lusty flame of passion and romance every woman dreamed of finding.

She settled in a comfortable chair and pulled the bassinet close. "Have your other guests left?"

"All but one couple. They're at the tennis courts playing doubles with our men."

Gareth's mother's reference was so casual, Stacy almost missed the impact of it. When she realized what Mrs. Clelland had said, she protested. "Gareth isn't mine."

"He is if you want him." Mrs. Clelland whirred frozen orange juice and water in a blender. She brought a glass to Stacy. "Coffee?" She was walking on her injured ankle.

"Yes, please."

"You do want him, don't you?" Mrs. Clelland paused and shot her a piercing glance before going on with the meal.

With anyone else, Stacy would have found the conversation intrusive, but she knew Mrs. Clelland spoke from love of her son. "Yes, I want him," she admitted.

"Good. Be sure and tell him. Men are much more dense in affairs of the heart. Ah, here they are now." She beamed smiles on the noisy foursome who came into the kitchen, tennis rackets still in hand. "Who won?"

"Gareth and I beat the socks off them," the other woman said. She held up her racket in a victory sign, then set it in the corner and helped herself to a glass of orange juice.

The others did likewise, moving around the large kitchen perfectly at ease. Stacy subdued an unexpected burst of jealousy for the other woman, who was about Gareth's age and who didn't wear a ring or have the same last name as the man she was with.

The tennis players discussed the game with lots of laughter and teasing about each other's skill. The noise level in the kitchen went up several decibels, waking Billy. They stopped talking at his first wail of alarm.

"I'll take him to the nursery," Stacy said, wishing she'd been wise enough to leave him there in the first place.

She quickly wheeled the bassinet into the hall and down to the nursery. She placed the baby in the crib and tucked him in. When she sang a lullaby, he drifted into sleep once more.

Lingering beside the sleeping child, she decided she would call the child-care center the next day and arrange his keep. To leave him there each morning would tear her heart out...the way it would when she left Gareth and the law firm.

She didn't know where the thought came from, but once it settled into her mind, she knew that was what she would do. The passion between them was too strong to be denied if they stayed near each other. She wouldn't accept him on those terms. Her love was worth more than that.

With a troubled sigh, she left the quiet room and returned to the kitchen. The table was set and part of the group had taken their seats. She resumed her former place.

Gareth brought a Mexican platter of bacon and sausage links and placed it in the center of the table. His father brought the first round of waffles while Mrs. Clelland started a new batch.

The scene exuded an innocent charm similar to a Norman Rockwell painting. *Breakfast in the Country,* it could be titled. Tears filmed her eyes. She blinked them away.

The chair beside her moved, then Gareth sat down and pulled closer to the table. His arm brushed hers, the sun-bleached hairs tickling her skin. She laid her arm in her lap.

"Bacon or sausage?" he asked and held the platter for her.

She took two pieces of bacon. He helped himself and passed the food to his right.

His body radiated a steady warmth. She leaned toward him, wanting to absorb as much as possible. Her heart-beat quickened, sending the thin, hot blood pounding through her.

Gareth forked a waffle on her plate, then his. "One enough?" he asked.

His voice flowed over her, warm and deep, as smooth as melted butter. She nodded and reached for the juice, needing something to cool her off. Her eyes met those of the woman who sat opposite her. Ruthie, Stacy recalled the name.

Ruthie looked from her to Gareth and back. In an instant, Stacy knew the other woman had wanted him, but had given it up as hopeless long ago. Now she was wondering what he saw in Stacy.

Stacy wondered, too, when she risked a glance in his direction. He was watching her with the same stark intensity she had noticed before. It made her tremble. Again he didn't appear to be aware of the flames that glowed in his eyes, making her ache with longing for the promises contained in those depths.

"You slept late," he said in a low tone while his mother discussed the success of the auction with the others. "I missed our game."

"You had plenty of competition and an able partner."

He glanced at the other female guest, then back to her. "But she wasn't as much fun to watch."

Stacy's breath jumbled into a knot.

"And I shouldn't be saying this," he concluded, a brief frown appearing on his face, his laughter mocking his own actions. He shook his head as if disgusted with his lack of control. "You need milk," he announced. He rose and proceeded to pour her a glass and bring it to her.

There was a lull in the general conversation. Four pairs of eyes noted the thoughtful gesture with varying expressions reflected in them. His parents beamed approval, his mother joyful, his father thoughtful. Ruthie's eyes gleamed with dislike. The male guest eyed her in an interested fashion. The attention made Stacy nervous.

She mumbled a thank you and kept her eyes on her plate. When the meal was over, she jumped to her feet and cleared the table. Gareth rinsed and stored the dishes in the dishwasher.

Mrs. Clelland played the invalid to perfection. She had her husband bring a pillow and prop her bound ankle on a chair. "We have time for a lecture at the museum," she said. "Do you want to attend with us, or do you have to rush off?" she asked the visiting couple.

Gareth's mouth turned up ever so little at the corners. He wanted them gone. Stacy kept a carefully straight face even as she fervently hoped they'd leave.

"We have to be going," Ruthie answered without waiting for her escort's reply.

"Yes," the man echoed.

Stacy realized she hadn't caught his name. Not that it mattered. She wasn't going to be part of their circle of friends anyway. She didn't want to be.

By the time she and Gareth had the kitchen finished, his parents had retired to their room to dress. The other two had packed and said their farewells in a surprisingly short time.

Gareth poured fresh coffee into their cups and took his place at the table. He picked up a section of the paper and began reading. She did the same.

After his parents left, he laid the paper aside and studied her. His perusal made her nervous. She finally gave up on trying to concentrate and, holding her cup in front of her like a shield, returned his look.

"What is it?" she asked.

"Are you as glad to be alone as I am?"

"Yes."

His eyes roamed over her face, stopping at her eyes, the curly wisps of hair at her temples that had escaped the combs, then landing on her lips. "What bothered you about them?"

Startled, she jerked the cup, sloshing the coffee over the rim. She mopped up the splatter with a napkin. "I don't know what you mean."

"I think you do," he countered softly.

She stared into the steam rising off the surface before facing him again. "I wouldn't like to be part of a couple like them. They...there was no commitment between them. The weekend was a casual thing of no consequence."

"Adults today don't need a lot of false promises to be able to enjoy themselves and each other."

"I wouldn't want false promises, either, but I would expect to love the man I slept with."

"Would you expect the same from him?" The sardonic twist in the question conveyed his thoughts loud and clear.

She answered truthfully. "Yes."

His dark eyebrows drew toward each other until a nick appeared over the bridge of his nose while he considered the situation. He rubbed a finger around the rim of his cup.

She loved his hands—broad, long-fingered hands. Big hands. Steady hands. The hands of a good man.

Turning her head, she watched the morning sun sparkle off the grassy sweep of lawn until she could trust herself not to leap into his arms and demand he love her.

Gareth knew the moment Stacy turned her attention from him. He fought an impulse to reach over and tilt her head back in his direction. More than anything, he wanted to punish her mouth with his, to chastise her for making him want her with every fiber of his being. Yeah, some punishment.

He didn't want to want a woman. Like a limb that's been asleep, his heart throbbed painfully whenever he thought of Stacy. He didn't like yearning for her, listening for her voice and her laughter to the exclusion of all others. Most of all, he didn't like the fact that he felt alive only when she was near. He'd been through that turmoil, the death that wasn't death although he'd wished it had been....

He didn't want to think about it.

A smooth hand slid over his, rubbing until he relaxed his grip on the cup. He watched as she moved her hand along his arm until she arrived at his shoulder. Standing, she stepped behind him and massaged the muscles of his neck and shoulders.

Don't touch me, he wanted to say. "Don't stop," he said.

"Your muscles are so tight." She bent forward as she murmured to him, her voice as caressing as her hands.

Ah, God, it was pain. It was torment. It was wonderful.

"Why?" he groaned even as he melted under her care.

"Why what?" she asked, almost on a whisper.

He grappled with his control, but the words came out anyway. "Why did you let me hold you and kiss you?"

She was silent so long, he'd decided she wasn't going to answer the stupid question. "I think you know," she finally said, so low he had to strain to hear.

He turned and pulled her across his lap, his arms locking around her of their own volition. He was past thinking, past caring about pain or memories or nightmares. He had to touch her. It was as necessary as air.

Stacy was stunned at the impact of his kiss. His mouth closed on hers as if punishing her for the desire that bloomed like a sturdy weed between them no matter how hard either of them tried to keep it from sprouting.

Thoughts fled as the kiss became deeper, more demanding. His hand in her hair, the arm around her shoulders, locked her against him until there was no space left to think. There was only this terrible need that burned in her, hot and desperate.

The tears seeped out from under her closed eyelids. They ran down her cheeks into the corners of her mouth. She knew the exact moment he felt them.

He eased the pressure of his mouth, then kissed his way to the corner of her mouth. There, he sipped the salty tears from her lips, then licked them from her cheeks, first one side, then the other. He was so exquisitely gentle.

She fought the turbulent emotions until her control was once more assured. The tears stopped.

He licked her lashes clear of the last drops, then raised his head and studied her. "Why are you crying?"

"I don't know."

The silence stretched between them. She laid her head on his shoulder and remembered another time when she'd done the same. When she'd arrived at his cabin, his eyes hadn't been welcoming. They weren't now.

His hands were gentle, but his soul wasn't. He hated it that he wanted her. He hated the passion between them. Did it follow that someday he would grow to hate her?

He sighed and stood, making sure she was steady on her feet before releasing her.

"I'd like to go home," she requested. Weariness folded around her like a mist.

"Emotion is exhausting, isn't it?"

She started at his insight. "Very."

"My mother will have lunch and the afternoon planned. Can you make it until this evening?"

She summoned the last of her reserves. "Of course."

"Of course," he repeated. He touched her cheek, then dropped his hand to his side. "You would inspire a saint."

"Hardly. My response to you—" She stopped, realizing what she was about to say.

"Isn't saintly?" he suggested.

She met his eyes. "No."

"Neither is mine to you." He thrust his hands into the pockets of his tennis shorts and strode to the door. He went outside, his stride long as he walked away.

Her eyes were drawn to the solid length of his legs. She'd felt those rock hard muscles against her thighs. She knew the strength in his arms. She loved the warmth of his body. He was an ideal man, capable of great kindness as well as great passion, but only he could choose to share those traits with another.

* * *

"Clelland and Davidson," Stacy said into the phone. She eyed the stack of mail still be opened.

"Stacy, this is Shirl. Guess where I am?"

"Well, you're not at your desk, nor were you yesterday. Pete is fuming, Gareth is irritated, and I'm swamped with work."

"I'm married."

"You're what?" Stacy couldn't keep her voice from rising in a stunned shriek.

"Married. I . . . we eloped."

"Who . . . you're not seeing anyone . . . Shirl, are you all right?"

Laughter rolled over the telephone line. "My pilot. We're in Mexico. Tell the boss men I'm taking the week off."

"Heaven help us," Stacy muttered. "Gareth will kill you. Right after Pete does."

Shirl wasn't worried. "Wish me luck?"

Stacy heard the wistful note in her friend's tone. "You know I do, the very best of luck and everything else. You deserve it."

"Now I'm getting all teary-eyed. Oh-oh, here comes the groom. I'll call you as soon as I get home. Oh, you'll need to find a new secretary. I'm giving notice. I'll be moving to Houston in a couple of weeks."

The door between the offices opened. Gareth stepped into the doorway and watched Stacy as she finished the conversation. They'd hardly spoken in the eight days since he'd brought her home from the weekend at his parents' farm.

"Shirl is married," she told him, replacing the phone. "She's in Mexico, married to a pilot. She's moving to Houston."

"You look stunned. I take it this was a complete surprise?"

"Yes. She told me she wasn't seeing him anymore."

He shrugged. "She changed her mind. A woman's prerogative."

Stacy pressed a hand to her stomach, which felt as if she'd swallowed a fist-size rock.

"What's different today?" he suddenly asked. He glanced around the office, a frown deepening on his face.

"There's no baby stuff," she said quickly. "Billy went to the day-care center this morning."

Gareth strolled around her office, looking at the plants and her personal touches as if seeing them for the first time. "How did he take to it? Aren't babies supposed to have some time to adjust before you leave them all day at a new place?"

His eyes narrowed on her. She licked her lips, feeling like a witness on the stand. "I stopped by after work each day last week so he would become used to the surroundings and the woman who will take care of him. I spent half a day there on Saturday and let him wake up with me out of sight. He did fine."

Gareth frowned as if displeased.

She resumed slitting envelopes and checking the mail, which normally was Shirl's job. She'd already delegated several chores among the four typists and collected the reports of the four law students who were working for the firm this semester on a work-study program with the University of Virginia. The office was running almost smoothly.

"My mother asked about you and the boy," he said, pausing at the side of her desk. "She said it livened up the house to have a young one about."

"Please thank her for me." Stacy looked over a letter, laid it in the correct pile and picked up another one. She cleared her throat. "You remember Mr. Anders, my old boss who retired?"

"Yes."

"His son, the one that's a policeman...was a policeman...has started his own investigation agency."

"A private eye? We might use him sometime."

"He investigates insurance fraud and apparently has all the business he can handle. He wants me to come to work for him."

There, she'd gotten the words out without fainting. It was a move she'd been contemplating for five days.

"No," Gareth stated.

She frowned up at him. He stepped closer, looming over her, large and mean-eyed and short-tempered.

"You don't want to get mixed up in anything like that. It's too dangerous," he informed her.

"Actually, I'll be running the office while he and his partner do the investigating. It sounds like...fun." And that sounded like the lamest excuse for leaving she'd ever heard. "It would be closer to the nursery school. I could have lunch there and nurse Billy, too."

"You can do that now. Take a longer lunch. I told you he could stay here until he gets too big. Why did you put him in the day-care center?"

"I thought it was best for him to get used to it before he got old enough to really notice his surroundings."

"Well, I don't."

Her hackles rose at his imperious manner. "Well, I do."

He glared until he realized she wasn't going to back down. Turning abruptly, he ran a hand through his hair and muttered under his breath.

"I beg your pardon?" she said icily.

"You ought to," he snapped, spinning around. "I'm not surprised at Shirl's actions, but I expected more loyalty from you. Here we are in a crisis and you're going to walk out."

"Well, not right away. I mean . . . I will give notice. A month . . ." At his fierce glare, she added, "Maybe six weeks."

"Thanks." Sarcasm dripped from the word.

She lifted her chin. "I'll find someone and train her—"

"The hell you will! You're staying and that's that!" He stomped toward the door.

"I meant, to take Shirl's place. I'll call the employment agency today."

"For Shirl's replacement?"

"Yes."

"Good. I'm not accepting a resignation from you," he told her in a voice that rumbled like distant thunder, foretelling a storm just beyond the horizon. He stepped into his office and slammed the door. The glass rattled dangerously.

Stacy propped her chin on her hand and went over every word of the conversation. She couldn't figure him out. He obviously hated to have anything to do with her, yet he wouldn't let her leave. Did that make sense?

Stacy hung up the phone and sighed in relief. It had been a frantic week, but she had a replacement for Shirl lined up. The woman had worked for a judge who'd had a heart attack and decided to retire. She could start Monday. Shirl, due in from her honeymoon, could give the new secretary a week's training and then leave to join her husband.

And so it goes, as some news commentator used to say.

After stretching and yawning, Stacy turned off the computer and printer and locked her desk. Maybe she' stop for a pizza on the way to the nursery and have that for dinner. A plain cheese one shouldn't flavor her milk so that Billy wouldn't eat.

Her son was growing and seemed happy in his new environment. Once more she concentrated her love on him and refused to think about Gareth and what might have been.

No regrets, she told herself firmly. Her love wasn't wanted. It would die a natural death soon.

She fetched the copper watering can from the top of the file cabinet and went to the ladies' room to fill it. When she returned to her office, Gareth was there.

"Hello," she said brightly. "You got back early. Did the case close or is this a recess?"

"We finished. Got a nice settlement, too." He mentioned the figure, shrugged, then spoiled the nonchalant act by grinning. Stacy knew how much he liked to win.

"Wow," she exclaimed. The firm would receive a six-figure fee. Of course they'd spent a lot on research and expert witnesses. Still, the net would be a goodly amount.

"I feel like celebrating. How about dinner?"

Her heart bounced off her rib cage before settling down to a regular beat again. "I have to pick up Billy," she said, injecting just the right amount of friendly regret in the refusal. "I think I'll stop for pizza on the way."

"I'll get it."

She finished her chore and replaced the copper can on the cabinet before answering. "I don't think that's a good idea."

"Why?"

"Because." She glared at him. He knew the answer to that as well as she did. They had to maintain a distance until they got over the insane passion they had for each other.

"I'd like to talk to you," he said after the silence grew to unbearable lengths.

"What about?"

"Life," he suggested philosophically.

She didn't trust him in this strangely mellow mood. "Yeah, right. It stinks, end of discussion."

Picking up her purse from the credenza by the window, she dropped her office keys into the side pocket. She watched the traffic eight stories down, her mind lingering on the dinner offer.

Behind her, she heard him pacing about the office, restless and probably irritated with her for refusing his invitation. He liked to get his own way and did so far too often.

Her mood turned to anger with herself for wanting things she wasn't going to get. She grabbed the strap of her purse and swung it over her shoulder.

Her fist connected with warm, living flesh.

"Damn!" her boss said and pressed a hand over his eye.

"Don't move," she ordered. "I'll get some cold water. Give me your handkerchief."

He handed it over. She rushed to the fountain in the hall and soaked it with the icy cold water. After wringing enough water out so it wouldn't drip, she ran to the office.

Gareth was seated in her chair, his hand still over his eye.

"Here," she said. She pushed his hand away and placed the cold cotton over his eye. She watched him anxiously.

"That's better," he murmured.

"I don't understand," she mused aloud. "How did I hit you? I mean, why were you bending over my shoulder?"

"Smelling your perfume."

"I don't wear perfume to work."

"I know." He sighed heavily. "I like your hair up like that. It makes you look sweet and young. I wanted to kiss the back of your neck."

Stacy's hand flew to the twist on the back of her head. She'd twigged the hair up to keep it out of the way. Billy was forever pulling on it when she left it in his reach.

"You were going to kiss the back of my neck?" she demanded incredulously.

"Yes." He cast her a resentful glance from his good eye.

"Well, you can't. Not in the office. It isn't...it isn't dignified," she spluttered.

"Spare me the lecture."

"You can't go around kissing someone's neck just because you want to. You're not allowed to do that. It's against the regulations of the...the Equal Opportunity Office."

His snort of laughter was cruel. "You can kiss my neck. What could be fairer?" Now he was acting his usual cynical self.

"This isn't funny!" She realized her purse was still hanging on her shoulder. "I can't stand here arguing about it. I have things to do."

She stomped out of the office. He could think again if he thought he could kiss her whenever he wanted. She wasn't that kind of woman. She wouldn't fall into his arms just because he wanted her to. Even if she had each time he'd touched her in the past. But no more.

She arrived home and changed clothes, then fed Billy before she remembered she'd forgotten her pizza. That made her angry all over again. Damn Gareth Clelland and his kisses!

Billy patted her breast while he nursed. Her mood softened. Such a sweet baby. "How I love you," she whispered. "You make everything worthwhile."

Gareth had no one to make life worthwhile for him. He would grow old and callous, maybe become the type of man who thought he could take what he wanted without consequences. He would use his charm and money and influence to replace the ravages of time and dissipation on his handsome face and strong body.

Such a waste.

She shook her head in pity for what she imagined he would become. He had so much potential—as a lover and a husband.

A sigh escaped her. To find in a man the steady flame that could warm a marriage through all the years, to discover that same flame could erupt into a passion so intense it lifted her to the stars, and not to be able to claim it...

Life could be so unfair.

Chapter Nine

Stacy turned off the computer and picked up the employee review forms from the printer rack. She read them over word for word, determined to spot any typos or errors before Gareth pointed them out to her. Everything was in order.

Putting the papers on her desk, she glanced at the clock. Her boss was due back in the office any time. She'd penciled in an appointment for herself to go over the employee raises with him, then she planned on leaving early, if possible.

It was Tuesday, May 11. Her son had been born three months ago today. Only three months, yet she could barely remember a time when he hadn't been part of her life. The biggest part.

Her breasts tightened a little as usual when she thought of the baby. She adjusted her bra to a more comfortable position.

The outer door opened. Gareth entered the office, filling it with his masculine presence. He looked extraordinarily handsome in a blue summer suit with a hint of gray stripe. His shirt was dark red, and his tie combined the three colors.

Her nipples contracted into hard points. Thank heavens for nursing pads which disguised the fact. "Hi," she said brightly. "You're right on time. I have the employee evaluations ready."

She rose, ready to follow him into his office. He stopped and looked her over as if she were an intrusive stranger. "I have a couple of calls to make."

"Yell when you're finished," she requested. "I'm planning on leaving early tonight, if possible." She'd been late getting out three nights that week.

He made a sound in his throat that might have been agreement. Or then again, it might not. He went into his office and closed the door.

She set her lips primly together and placed the papers back on the pristine surface of her desk. A minute later, she heard him on the phone. An hour dragged by.

When he hung up, she grabbed her forms and headed for his door. It opened wide just as she grasped the knob. She was yanked forward and off balance. Gareth's arms shot out, catching her against him as she fell.

Shaking the hair back from her face, she gazed at him in stunned surprise. Then sensation poured over her like a summer rain shower. She felt the rise and fall of his chest against her breasts. His thigh was wedged between hers. His arms enclosed her with rock solid strength.

Against her abdomen, she felt the rapid hardening of his body. Her eyes widened in shock while desire surrounded her in tentacles of warmth.

In the taut silence that followed, their joint breaths were the only sound. Like track stars who'd crossed the finish line and were hanging on to each other, she thought inanely.

She saw his eyes go to her mouth. Her lips were parted as she drew quick drafts of air into her lungs. Longing burst through her. She wanted him to kiss her and make the hurt of the past month go away.

He licked his lips, his gaze narrowing as if reading her mind. Slowly his head lowered. Their lips had almost touched when a knock on the outer door froze them in place.

"Yo," Pete called. He opened the door and walked in. And stopped dead still.

Stacy's mind went completely blank.

Gareth muttered a curse and stepped back, his arms falling away from her. He whirled on his law partner. "What is it?"

Pete held up both hands as if to ward off danger. "I thought we were supposed to meet in the conference room an hour ago to go over the employee evaluations with Stacy. Did I get the wrong date?" He looked from one to the other.

Stacy began functioning again. "No. You're right. We . . . I was just going to remind Gareth of the meeting."

"Well, then, are we ready to begin?" Pete asked, his expression neutral while his gorgeous blue eyes gleamed with laughter. "I have a hot date tonight."

She stared at the papers in her hand. "Uh, yes. Yes, I have the forms. I just finished them a while ago."

"You two go ahead," Gareth ordered. "I'll bring some coffee and join you in a minute."

She nodded. Feeling as stiff as a new robot, she crossed Gareth's office and entered the private conference room.

She took a seat at the gleaming walnut table and laid copies of the evaluation forms at two other places.

Pete came in and took a seat. He gave her a careful once-over, then picked up the papers and began studying them.

Heat suffused her face. Gareth had nearly kissed her. Another inch and their mouths would have joined. And she hadn't made one protest. Not one.

What had they been thinking—to almost kiss right there in the office?

Obviously, neither of them had thought at all. They had reacted mindlessly to each other. Both of them. Gareth as well as her. What had happened to common sense?

Gareth entered the conference room from his office. He carried three cups of coffee, which he set on the table, then pushed one to her and one to Pete.

"Thank you," she murmured. Her voice was so husky, she had to clear it twice. She felt her face grow hotter.

"Yeah, thanks." Pete took a sip from the plastic cup. "I've looked over the recommendations you made," he said to her. "I don't have any problems with them."

Gareth slouched into a chair. He'd taken off his jacket and tie. His collar was open and his shirtsleeves were rolled up on his forearms. The room was silent while he perused the forms.

"How's the new secretary working out?" he asked when he finished. He looked at her.

"She's very competent and is already finding her way around. She's familiar with law terms. I plan on recommending a raise for her at the end of her first three months."

"All right. These others look fine to me." He glanced at Pete. "You want to handle the next one?"

"Nah, you can do the honors. It's after five, and I need to leave." He stood, pushed the chair in with his foot and headed for the door. With a smile at her, he left.

Stacy realized the outer offices were silent. The typists, law clerks and new secretary had left. The blood slowed to a sluggish crawl through her veins. She felt dull-witted, her body heavy with needs she constantly had to deny.

"Pete and I are pleased with your management skills. The office functions well under your leadership. A tight ship and a happy one. We decided a ten percent raise was in order."

She blinked in surprise. "You've already given me two raises," she reminded him. "One at three months and one at the end of my first year."

He shrugged. All trace of the earlier desire was wiped from his eyes. He was the cool, impersonal boss, always polite, but rarely smiling. "I suppose if you don't want it, we can't make you take the extra money. We figured you could use it since you have two to feed."

"Of course I can use it." She fidgeted with the papers. "I don't want charity from you."

Anger settled like a cloud on his handsome features. "Charity isn't on our list of employee benefits," he told her in a voice straight off an Arctic ice floe. "You earned it."

"Thank you." She stood. "If that's all..."

He rose, his greater height making her feel small and stupid and helpless for some reason she couldn't name. Then the most ridiculous thing happened. Tears filmed her eyes.

Horrified by this emotional stumble, she said good-night and rushed out of the room. Back in her own office, she locked up, grabbed her purse and headed out the door before she disgraced herself completely.

She nearly ran over Pete when she lunged into the elevator before the door closed. "Easy," he said, catching her arm to steady her. She smiled weakly and regained her composure. "I didn't want to wait for the next elevator."

"I noticed." His eyes studied her face.

She pushed a smile on her lips. "Thank you for the raise. It was a nice surprise, I must say."

"You're worth it. You handle twice the load of our last assistant. The office has never run better."

"Thank you." She couldn't think of another word. The elevator swooped downward with a soft swish of cables and gears.

"How's the boy doing?"

"Fine. Growing like a weed."

"Good." The door slid open, and they exited into the parking garage. "I'll walk you to your truck." He fell into step beside her. "Are you happy here with us?"

"Of course."

"Now that you've got the polite answer out of the way, tell the truth—are you happy working with us?"

She stopped by the ute and unlocked the door. "I don't know what you want me to say."

"Gareth has been a bear lately, especially to you. A few minutes ago, I'm pretty sure he was about to kiss you. When are you going to put the poor guy out of his misery?"

"H-how?" She hated the telltale catch.

"Well, let's see." Pete's eyes sparkled as he pretended to figure it out. "If he's asked you to marry him, then I think you should . . . for all our sakes."

She gasped, then snapped her mouth shut.

"If he's suggested something more casual, then tell him it's marriage or nothing. Turn in your resignation. That'll wake him up." The law partner chuckled with delight. "I'll hire you as a paralegal assistant if he doesn't come through. You know as much about the law as most of us legal eagles.''

"My father was an attorney. I stayed at the office with him after school and in the summer after my mother died."

"What are you going to do about Gareth?"

"I don't know."

"Well, you two are going to have to work it out," he said seriously. "I'm afraid there's going to be an explosion soon. I hope it doesn't happen at the office. If it does, I think you'll have to pack up and leave. No hard feelings, but he's my partner. I have to work with him. You're the expendable one." He gave her a sympathetic smile.

"I understand." She climbed in the ute. He closed the door, the smile hovering on his lips. She managed to return it.

She worried over the situation on the way to the day-care center and all the way home. At bedtime, she still hadn't hit upon a course that would allow her to remain at the law firm. Pete was right. The situation was too volatile.

After changing clothes, she sat in the rocker and fed the baby while she faced the truth. She would have to leave. The new secretary was an older woman with over twenty years business experience under her belt. She could take over the running of the office with no problem.

The detective, her old boss's son, had called and begged her to think about his offer. The secretary they had wasn't working out. He couldn't offer her as much money as she was presently making, but he'd promised her a bonus at the end of the year if the company continued to do as well as it was now.

Choices. Life was full of them.

Her son made a gurgling sound. She smiled at him. He let go the nipple and gave her a milky smile in return.

Three months old. It seemed like a lifetime ago—her going to the cabin, getting lost, having the baby, Gareth taking care of them.

Her smile became wobbly. She beat back tears by dint of will. "We'll be okay," she promised her son. "We can make it just fine. We don't need anyone else."

But Gareth would make a wonderful father, insisted some stubborn part of her that wouldn't give up the dream.

The resignation was typed and ready. All Stacy had to do was lay it on Gareth's desk. Or she could give it to Pete.

Coward.

Gareth had hired her as his assistant. More and more duties had been added to her list until she'd ended up managing the whole office, but Gareth was her boss.

Remembering his fury when she'd mentioned quitting when Shirl had left and his uncertain temper of late, he might strangle her on the spot when he saw the resignation. The other job was waiting for her. She had to give two weeks notice, but after that, she'd be out of there and out of his life.

She heard him enter his office. She stuck the letter in a file folder like a thief hiding her loot. Later. She'd give it to him later. As soon as she found out what kind of a mood he was in. She'd been waiting all week for his temper to improve. It hadn't. Today was Friday. She had to do it today.

She checked the letters one of the typists had finished and placed it in the folder. The will was finished. She handled most of the estate work like this, getting it put together with all the clauses and whereases and such. All Gareth needed to do was to look it over, then she would call the client to come in and sign it—

The door between their offices jerked open. Gareth scowled at her. "Where's the Lambridge file?"

"Right here."

"I need it." He strode across the short distance like a hungry bear smelling fresh meat, grabbed the folder and returned to his den.

"You're quite welcome," she muttered at the closed door. She repositioned the combs in her hair while sneaking a glance at her watch. Fifteen minutes to go. Thank God.

She'd slip her letter of resignation under his door and run like mad for the elevator. She frowned in disgust at her lily-livered ways.

Restless, she went out and told Pat and the typists goodnight and wished them a pleasant weekend. The law interns had already left. And Pete, of course.

When the room was empty, she rushed back to her office. Now was the time to make her getaway. She grabbed her purse, wrote Gareth's name on an envelope and picked up the letter.

Except it wasn't her letter. It was instructions on the will from their client.

She stared at her desk. It was the only piece of paper on its smooth surface. She pressed a hand to her stomach while suspicion bloomed like poison ivy in her mind.

Oh, no. She hadn't. Please, no—

"*Stacy, get in here.*" The roar shook the glass pane in the door between his office and hers.

She'd put her letter in the folder, the one he'd snatched off her desk. He was going to kill her. With fatalistic calm, she crossed the carpet and entered the bear's den.

"Yes?" She folded her arms over her rock-filled tummy and held herself very still.

He gave her the absolutely meanest look she'd ever received from him...or anyone. "What is the meaning of this?" He waved a sheet of white bond paper at her.

"What is it?" she asked. Maybe he'd found a mistake in the will. Maybe he hadn't seen her letter.

"You know what the hell it is."

Oh. He had found it. "My...uh...resignation?"

"Yes." He gave her a lethal stare. "I thought we'd had this conversation two or three weeks ago. I thought we'd resolved this particular matter at that time."

"Yes, we did, and no, we didn't." She thrust out her chin. She wasn't going to cower like a thief caught in the act.

His scowl could have downed a moose at twenty paces.

"We didn't resolve it...not exactly," she added.

"What exactly did we do?"

Witnesses must hate it when he used that soft growl to question them. It contained hidden mines that they knew were going to explode in their faces. Stacy felt the same.

"Well, we sort of left it open. The policeman, the one who started the detective agency, called again. He really needs someone in his office."

"How much is he paying you?"

"Uh..."

His eyes narrowed to silver stilettos. "He isn't paying you as much as we are." He watched her without blinking. *"Is he?"* he suddenly barked.

Every nerve in her body jumped. "No!"

"I thought not. So what's your excuse for this?" He waved the incriminating paper at her.

She blurted the truth. "I thought it would be better if I left since things were sort of...tense...between us." Tense was the least offensive word she could think of. Dangerous or explosive or deadly might be more descriptive.

"No," he said. He tore the paper in half. Then half again. And again. And threw the pieces in the trash can.

She was so angry, her voice shook. "You can't do that."

"I just did."

"I'll print out another one."

"We're going to waste a lot of paper."

She stared at him for one long, furious, confused minute. "Blast you," she said and whirled and left the office.

All the way down the elevator, she expected him to be waiting when she stepped out. He wasn't. She peered around cautiously, then dashed to the truck like the coward she was.

Once locked inside, she cranked the engine and left with a squeal of rubber on the concrete. On the street, she slowed as she merged with the heavy traffic.

Breathing easier, she considered the situation. She'd turned in her resignation. No matter what he said or did with it, it was valid. She knew her rights. Gareth Clelland wasn't going to intimidate her. She might not work out the two weeks.

So there.

After picking up Billy, she stopped at the grocery, then hurried home, anxious to be inside the safety and solitude of her apartment. Again she kept a sharp eye out for her boss as she rode the elevator up to her floor. No one there.

Sighing in relief, she let herself in, then flicked the dead bolt when she closed the door.

Safe at last.

Gareth paced the hallway, unable to make up his mind whether to knock on Stacy's door or go home and let the situation ride until Monday morning at the office.

Of course, she might not come in at all.

He stopped at the wall ten feet from her door and looked down into the street. Friday night traffic crawled along like a loosely connected caterpillar with lights on each section.

"Damn," he said, slapping the wall with the flat of his hand. He spun around and headed for the door.

Without giving himself time to think about why he was there and what possible ulterior motives he might have in coming over here at night instead of waiting for the formality of Monday and the office, he rang the doorbell.

No answer.

He tried once more.

No answer.

"Dammit," he said aloud. He banged the door with his knuckles and heard the faint wail of the baby. Ah, she was in.

But she didn't come to the door.

Fury overcame his better sense. He pounded the door with three hard raps. "Stacy, I know you're in there. Now open the damned door before I break it in," he bellowed.

The elevator doors opened. A couple stood there looking shocked to the gills.

"Got a crowbar?" he asked with a nasty smile.

The man shook his head. The woman pressed a hand to her bosom, her eyes about to pop out of her head. Gareth reached up to knock once more.

The door opened. Velvety brown eyes glared at him. His heart lurched like a drunk baboon. Stacy wore shorts, a loose T-shirt, and no shoes. The baby was cupped against her chest. She personified feminine beauty.

The couple on the elevator stayed there. "Do you need us to call the police?" the man asked, giving Gareth a wary glance.

"No, it's okay. Really," she added when they didn't look reassured. "He's my—"

"Tooth fairy," Gareth supplied. He stepped inside the apartment, closed the door and threw the dead bolt for good measure. He and Stacy were going to have a long talk.

"That wasn't funny," she told him, turning her back and retreating to the kitchen. She checked a Crock-Pot on the counter by the stove.

Her shorts were the type used for jogging. They had slits cut up the sides so they wouldn't bind across the thighs. Her legs were good. He'd noticed that often enough. Her rear was rounded and fit his hands nicely when he'd caught her there and hauled her against him.

"That smells good." He was suddenly ravenously hungry. For food. For her. For anything she wanted to give him.

What did she want from him?

She stirred the ingredients, tasted the broth, then turned the pot off. "It's just pot roast."

He waited, knowing she was too polite to ignore him.

"Do you want some?" She was far from gracious.

"Yes."

She frowned, but didn't protest. She opened a cabinet and took two plates down with her free hand.

"Here, let me. Tell me what to do."

"Get the silver. In that drawer. Napkins there." She pointed them out.

He set the table, poured two glasses of milk and filled their plates with roast, potatoes, onions and carrots.

"Rolls in the oven." She placed the baby in a swing and wound up the spring. The merry tinkle of a nursery rhyme tune filled the room.

After finding an oven mitt, he removed two rolls and placed them on a saucer. He waited at the table for her to be seated before he took a chair opposite her. Their knees brushed when he stuck his legs under the table and pulled forward. She moved hers to the side.

"Weren't you going to answer the door?" he asked, cutting a slice of margarine from the stick and layering it on a roll. He did the same to the other one, placed it on the saucer and pushed it toward her plate, keeping one for himself.

"I didn't feel like arguing." She took a bite of roast, chewed and swallowed. "This is *my* time, you know."

"Yeah." He bit into a carrot, then closed his eyes in ecstasy. It was cooked to perfection, still firm, but done all the way through, sweet and tasty. The meat was falling-apart tender. He mashed the potato with his fork and added more gravy from the Crock-Pot. "You want more gravy?"

"No, thank you." She ate primly, one hand in her lap clutching the napkin, the other tucked close to her side as she ate in small, ladylike bites.

Her hair was pulled into a loose ponytail, making her neck bare. He had to fight a strong urge to kiss her there.

Returning to the table, he turned his appetite on the food. It was so damned good. He ate firsts, then seconds, then after due consideration, had a small third helping.

"Off your feed, huh?" she suggested snidely.

He grinned, scooped up the last bite and put it away. "I was hungry." Now that he was inside with her and the boy, he felt much more relaxed. Happy, even. He stared at her mouth.

He liked watching her. She chewed daintily, with her lips pressed together, a frown of disapproval nicking two faint lines between her eyebrows. The lines would deepen with time.

In her fifties, she would fret about them. His mother had. She said they made a person look like a grouch. Now in her sixties, she no longer worried about a few lines.

"Do the women in your family age fat or thin?" he asked.

She looked at him over the rim of her milk glass. After swallowing the last sip, she patted her mouth with the napkin. "I don't know. My mother was in her thirties when she died. I never knew either of my grandmothers."

"Too bad," he murmured.

She immediately looked suspicious of his sympathy.

He wasn't going to win her that way. Win her? He wanted her to return to work. That was all. He watched her wipe her mouth and recalled how soft her lips could be.

"Did you drop by to discuss family genetics?"

"No." He pushed his plate back with a sigh of satisfaction and crossed his arms on the table. "I came to apologize for my behavior at the office. Your resignation took me by surprise."

She gave him an uncompromising stare.

"However, I didn't have the right to tear it up."

"No, you didn't."

"I'll miss you." He glanced toward the swing. "I already miss the boy."

"His name is Billy."

"Yeah. William Bainbridge Gardenas."

He witnessed the slow buildup of heat in her face when she realized he knew she'd named Billy after him as well as the baby's father. "I thought, after all I put you through that day, it was...it seemed the least I could do."

Gareth smiled at her stiff little speech. She was on the defensive. Good. Maybe it would give him a small advantage with her. She could be stubborn at times.

"It was an excellent thought. I was honored when I saw the birth announcement in the paper. Thank you."

"Oh. Well, you're welcome."

"My mother was pleased, too. Did she tell you?"

"No."

Very stubborn. "Will you stay at the office until we find someone else and get her trained?"

"Pat could take over easily. She's very capable."

His patience snapped, suddenly and without warning. "Dammit, I don't want Pat! I want you!" The thunder of his voice died away into the silent room.

"I want you," he said again, amazement filling him. A glow ignited inside him, like the sun coming up, warming the earth after a cold, dark night.

Somehow, without quite knowing how it happened, he was standing and she was standing. He reached right over and lifted her off the floor and into his arms.

He saw the protest forming on her lips. Before she could say it, he covered her lips with his.

Oh, God, she tasted good. Ambrosia. Honey. He sampled her with a wild roaming of his tongue on her lips, her teeth, in her mouth. He wanted a response. So far she was fighting it. That gave him hope.

"Stay," he mumbled against her mouth.

Her breasts heaved against his. Passion or anger? He didn't know.

He kept her busy with forays of his hands and mouth. She tried evasive tactics, then she became aggressive, trying to catch his hands and remove them, shaking her head from side to side to dislodge him. He held on, staying with her every move, feeling the glow grow hotter, the heat pouring out of him, surrounding them both, melting them together.

She freed her mouth and gasped for air. He pressed his face into her hair and breathed deeply of her—shampoo and cologne, the twin sweetness of baby powder and mother's milk.

"God, you smell good," he whispered, overcome with needs and emotions too strong to name. He couldn't. He'd never felt anything like this in his life. "We need to talk."

Taking her hand, he pushed her into her chair. For a minute, he stood there, his hands on her shoulders. Her smallness was deceptive. She had more inner strength than most men he knew.

He released her and paced about the kitchen. "I've been thinking about us for days . . . weeks."

Stacy raised her head and looked at him suspiciously.

"We've shared things this past year that a lot of people don't share in a lifetime." He searched her eyes. "Death. Birth. Desire."

She nodded. Her husband's death. The birth of her child. Desire from both of them. Her love for him, although he didn't know that. She folded her arms on the table and looked away.

He rubbed a fingertip along her jaw, then slipped it under her chin and caressed the sensitive skin there. "For most people, those things would form the basis of a solid friendship. For us, they seem to have raised a lot of problems. I think we need to solve them."

She couldn't think how.

"If I asked, would you be my lover?"

Every cell in her body went into suspended animation at the softly worded question. *My son is an honorable man. Take whatever he offers.* His mother's advice. Should she take it?

"Would you?"

"I don't know."

"We've nearly made love three times. That has to mean something, doesn't it?"

She shrugged as if her heart wasn't about to pound right out of her body.

"If I asked you to live with me, would you?"

She recoiled instinctively from the temporary nature of such a relationship. Her expectations were so much more.

"No."

"Then . . . perhaps we should consider marriage."

It was several seconds before she could think again.

"Yeah, I find the idea pretty daunting, too." He gave her a rather uncertain smile as if perplexed by the stormy relationship between them. "But I think it would work."

A chill flashed over her. "Do you?" He didn't catch the ice in her tone. "Why?"

He gave a ragged sigh and leaned both hands on the table. "I think about you all the time. I rush to the office just to see you. When you're near, all I want is to hold you and kiss you. It makes me angry when I can't. Before this grand passion, we used to work well together. I think marriage would solve several problems."

"I'm not like other women you've known. I'm not blasé about things like commitment or fidelity."

"Believe me, that won't be a problem." His smile was wry, conveying more than the words expressed.

She studied him, trying to arrive at a logical reason for this sudden offer of marriage.

"You're the only woman I've even wanted to touch in the past three years," he told her.

He had to be speaking rhetorically. "You've dated."

"Dated, yes. Nothing more. It's as if I'd died below the waist. Until you."

The impact of his words hit her. He hadn't made love to a woman since his fiancée died? No. She couldn't have understood him correctly. He was too sensuous, too virile and powerful...a handsome, healthy male who could have any woman he wanted.

"You can't mean...no women?"

"None."

He lifted her hand and kissed the tip of each finger, sending sparks up her arm and down into her abdomen. "At first, I wasn't sure what it was with you. That weekend at the cabin, I wanted to hold you. You were in my bed. I felt I should be there with you."

"You felt like that after the delivery?"

"Maybe it was insane, but yes, I did. I liked being with you. Sometimes it was peaceful. At others, it wasn't." His eyes blazed, reminding her of those times, not so peaceful, when their kisses had burned away any thoughts of self-preservation.

"Are you saying you love me?" She just couldn't believe this conversation.

"I find you sexy and exciting and very, very tempting. I want to make love to you. I've thought of those grandchildren we might give my mother. If that's love, then..." He left it for her to finish.

"You were in love once. You know what it's like."

His face closed. "I'll never feel like that again."

Cold and immediate, those words of denial. She flinched as if he'd slapped her.

"I didn't mean that," he said at once. "What I feel for you is hard to explain. I've never felt this way before. There's passion, but there's also admiration. I care for you. I'll be a good husband to you and a good father to your son. You know I'm a wealthy man. If something happens to me, you'll have enough money to live where and how you wish. Billy can go to Harvard—"

"No." She couldn't bear his logical, sensible explanation. "No more," she said, furious with him and with herself for letting herself hope.

"What is it?"

"You. This." She stood and moved away from him. "You intend to feel so much and no more. You'd parcel out your love like a miser." She shook her head. "It isn't enough."

Not when she knew the depth of tenderness that existed in him. Not when she could see the potential in him, the very force of life that he kept buried deep inside. She would eat her heart out for his complete love all the days of their marriage, and he might never share it with her.

His carefully drawn lines that she mustn't overstep would drive her insane. She could never be spontaneous in her love. She would forever be watching the boundaries. She loved him more than that. She wouldn't accept limitations.

"It isn't enough," she said again and faced the fury that bloomed in him.

"What is?" he demanded. "I've offered you my name, my money, a future of security for you and your son. What else do you want?"

She met his furious gaze. "I think you know."

He took a step toward her, then whirled and walked away. She listened to his steps in the hall, then the snick of the dead bolt as he opened the door. When the door closed, she sighed and looked at the swing.

A mother wasn't supposed to bawl like a kid. She had too many other things to do. "Poor baby," she murmured, bending over the sleeping child. "You've been such a good boy."

She froze in a half crouch, her arms reaching, but not touching. Something was wrong...very, very wrong. "Billy," she screamed. "Oh, God, no..."

Chapter Ten

Gareth heard Stacy's cry before he stepped more than a
foot away from the door. He froze for an instant, then
spun around and grabbed the doorknob, praying it didn't
have an automatic lock on it. It didn't. He raced to the
kitchen.

"Billy?" Stacy whispered.

Her voice sent a chill down his spine. He crossed the
room in four strides. "My God," he said.

Billy lay utterly still. His skin was white, like frostbite,
except around his lips and eyes. They were mottled with
blue. His hands, too.

She cradled him against her. "He's not breathing! Gareth, he's not breathing!"

"Bring him to the table." He slammed the dishes aside
with one sweep of his arm. A glass hit the floor but didn't
break.

She laid Billy down and opened his shirt. Gareth held
two fingers in the groove of the tiny neck. He finally de-

tected a beat, thready and weak. "Thank God, he has a pulse."

He licked his finger and held it under the boy's nose. No cooling effect of air passing over the wetness.

"Do you know CPR?" he asked.

"No. I don't."

"I do. You'll have to drive to the hospital. First we'll get some air into him."

Bending, he opened the rosebud mouth and put his lips over the baby's mouth and nose. The papery skin was smooth against his lips, as cool as tombstone marble. *Ah, God...*

He breathed into the boy's lungs in a short huff. Against his hand, he felt the thin rib cage lift. He raised his head and the air soughed out of the infant.

After ten breaths, the delicate eyelids faded from blue to white. Better. Billy wasn't breathing on his own, though.

"Get your keys," he told her. "Let's go."

They went down the elevator with him inhaling, huffing air into the tiny mouth, and exhaling the rest of the breath with the child. Stacy watched without a word, her face as white as her son's. Pity rose in him.

Inhale, huff, exhale.

In the ute, he ministered to the boy while she backed and drove out of the garage into the flow of Friday night revelers with the stoic courage of a warrior. *God...please...*

Inhale, huff, exhale.

The hot sting of tears shocked him. He knuckled them back with one hand. He could hardly bawl in front of her. She didn't need that from him. But inside, there was a tight, hurting sensation, as if some primal need gathered in upon itself. It coiled tighter, like a tiger crouching, ready to spring.

He forced the odd feelings at bay. There was no time for them. Billy grew cold to his touch. Gareth prayed one minute, cursed the next.

Inhale, huff, exhale.

Time condensed into this moment and this tiny human clasped in his hands. Next to the delicate limbs of the boy, his fingers felt like overgrown zucchini.

Inhale, huff, exhale.

They seemed no closer to the hospital than when they'd started. Billy lay limp on his lap, the matchstick arms and legs trailing along his thighs, shifting with each bounce of the ute as if they contained no bones at all.

The streetlights bled all color from the parchment-fine skin. Death caressed Gareth's neck with a sharp, ragged nail, flirting, teasing, mocking.

But he knew it was the boy that was wanted.

He locked his own fears inside and ached for Stacy. The control she displayed as she wove through the traffic, silent and courageous, tore at him.

Gareth lifted his head and swiped the sweat with his sleeve. Beneath his hand, the plum-size heart fluttered and skipped. The fragile connection between body and soul shredded until only a heartbeat held the torn threads intact.

He'd prayed before. For his dog to live after being hit by a car. For his grandfather to survive a heart attack. For Ginny to wake up and smile at him.

Now, as he placed his mouth over Billy's cool face, he prayed for Stacy and her son.

Please, God. Not Stacy. Don't do this to her.

He took a breath, huffed part of it into the boy's mouth, then lifted his head to release the rest of it. The air slipped from the blistery lips. None went in. He bent his head and willed life to remain.

I'll do anything. Anything. But don't take this child.
Inhale. Huff. Exhale.
I'll give her up.

Maybe it was too late for them anyway. He'd been a coward about her and the feelings they'd shared. Hurt once, he'd been afraid to trust life again. Stacy had lost her parents and her husband, yet she'd carried on without a whimper. She'd had her child and went on with living.

A man would be a fool to lose a woman like her.

The carefully guarded vaults of emptiness expanded and shattered. His heart filled with pity and anguish and the love he hadn't been able to admit. What a fool.

"We're here," Stacy said.

She wheeled into the semicircle of the emergency entrance, her hand on the horn blasting for help. She stopped at the curb. He was out of the ute before the engine quit running. Stacy was behind him by the time he ran through the sliding glass doors.

A male nurse shoved a gurney toward them. "What's the problem?" he asked, already reaching for the infant.

"He's not breathing," Gareth said. "I can't get him to breathe on his own."

"Right." The nurse called out a code.

In less than one minute, the medical team assembled. A doctor gave crisp orders.

Respirator. Heart monitor. IV.

Stacy stood by the white-tiled wall. The side of herself that was able to do what needed to be done in an emergency directed her movements. The other side screamed in silent fury at the unfairness of it all, at a fate that could allow this insult to her soul, this wound to her heart.

Gareth put his arm around her shoulders. She stood stiff and unyielding, the anger clutching at her throat, a mad thing clawing its way out. If she opened her mouth, she would scream.

"He'll be all right," he whispered to her.

She heard him, but she didn't believe him.

A big hand covered hers and rubbed gently at the fist she pressed to her stomach. She glanced at him.

Pity gleamed in his eyes. She sighed and let the anger go. "He has to be," she said simply. "He's all I've got."

The male nurse came over. "His heartbeat has picked up," he told them. His smile was cheery, as if this was news they'd been waiting for.

She nodded and tried to remember the miracles of modern medicine. Until the doctors told her differently, she had to believe her son would live.

"Is he breathing?" Gareth asked.

"Not on his own. Not yet." It would only be a matter of seconds, minutes at the most, his tone implied. "We're taking him to the ICU in Pediatrics. Fourth floor. There's a waiting room right outside the ICU main doors. You can go there."

A spurt of panic set in at the thought of them taking Billy away. She fought it back. "I want to go with my son."

The nurse was already walking off. "Soon," he called over his shoulder, taking a position beside the gurney. "As soon as we get him stabilized."

No, now, she wanted to say. She wanted to hold the tiny body that lay so pale against the faded green sheets of the gurney. She wanted to nurse him and make the life come back into him. When they wheeled him behind No Admittance doors, she trembled uncontrollably.

An arm closed around her waist. Gareth hauled her to him. "Let them do their job," he advised.

His strength flowed into her, firming her shaky legs. "I'm scared I'll never see him again," she told him.

"I know." He looked at her with such tenderness, she had to turn away.

A gray-headed woman bustled forward. "You'll need to sign the admitting forms."

"Where do we go?" Gareth asked.

"Through those doors. Admitting is on the right."

Gareth propelled her along. Her skin was icy to his touch. He hated the pain she was going through.

"It'll be okay," he said.

"Yes. Yes, of course it will." She managed a smile. It was so brave, it made him ache.

He guided her to the office, then answered the questions the girl behind the desk asked. The form was on the computer.

The admitting clerk was about twenty-two, bored with her job and indifferent to their suffering. Her long hair stuck out like a spiral mop around her head. The fluorescent lighting made her skin sallow, the blush on her cheeks magenta.

"Next of kin?" the girl asked, twiddling a corkscrew curl around and around one finger.

Gareth gave Stacy a little squeeze, telling her to answer.

"I am. I'm the next of kin," she said.

"Someone who doesn't live in the same household," the girl said. She clicked her artificial nails on the keyboard, impatient for the answer. "In case you skip out and don't pay the bill."

"There isn't anyone."

The girl shot her an irritated glance.

"I'll take care of it," Gareth broke in, his patience at the edge of control. He gave his name and address, his telephone number, the address of the office and the number there.

At last it was done. Stacy signed the forms.

"Let's go." Gareth swept her around and toward the bank of elevators next to the lobby.

Stacy felt his arm around her. His warmth enfolded her. She wanted to lean into it, but didn't dare. It would be that much worse when she had to stand on her own again. She knew just how wonderful he could be during a crisis, but she couldn't let herself depend on him.

In the waiting room, he ushered her to a seat, then brought coffee for each of them. It was hot. She set it aside.

After an hour, she stood and paced, moving from the door to the windows lining one wall. It was dark out. Night.

She leaned her forehead against the window. The heat of the day lingered in the glass, making it warm to her touch. She went back to the sofa and drank the lukewarm coffee.

"I'll see what I can find out," he said.

She nodded.

He left the room. After a while he came back. A doctor was with him, a woman with dark hair and soulful eyes, a kind smile in a tired face.

"He's stabilized," she told Stacy. The smile faded. "However, he hasn't started breathing on his own yet. I have a call in..."

Stacy saw the doctor's mouth moving, but she couldn't hear the words. At least it seemed that way. But she must because she knew what the woman was saying. Some research doctor had a new drug...a strong stimulus... could be dangerous...

More dangerous than not breathing?

". . . permission to use it. Would she sign the form?"

She signed a form. She'd already signed a bunch. She'd sign as many of the damned things as they wanted.

The doctor left.

Gareth seated her on the sofa and sat beside her. He pulled her close, folding her against him.

She resisted. He was warm. She was finding it harder to be strong and brave and all that. She wanted to wail.

"Stacy," he said. He sounded strange. So hoarse and strained. So sad. "Don't close me out." His hand crept up and cupped the side of her head. His arm tightened. "I know I deserve it, but don't shut me out. Let me share this with you."

His eyes were so sad. She reached up without thinking to soothe him. "It'll be okay," she said. She dropped her hand, having given as much as she could at the moment. There was so much sadness in his eyes, but she couldn't do anything about it.

"Ah, God," he breathed against her temple. His fingers kneaded her scalp.

Time passed. An hour. Another. Fear revived, becoming stronger. "Is my baby dead?" she asked.

"No, he isn't. His heart is beating." Gareth searched for words. People had said words to him when Ginny had died. Surely he could remember some of them.

They hadn't comforted him.

There must be others, some truth he could tell her. He found it. "He's got the strongest little heart. It just went on and on, beating like sixty. I breathed for him, but that heart . . . It keeps on and on."

"He's so little."

"He'll make it. His heart is like his mother's—too strong to give up, just like you've never given up on life no matter what it threw at you. Billy won't give up, either.'' He willed it to be so.

"He's such a good baby."

Her love broke his heart. He realized it was the same love she'd offered him, whole and complete.

She'd wanted the same from him. But he'd held back, thinking to give only a little of himself and so escape the greater pains of life. Love didn't work that way. A person had to take it all—the joy and the hurt.

Stacy understood. That's why she'd refused him.

"I know, love." He rubbed her, soothed her. He held her when she would have pushed him away. "He'll be okay. Have faith in him, in his heart. I do."

She leaned her head back on his arm so she could see his face. He held still and let her look into his eyes. She shook her head as if confused. She was too tired to understand the message he was trying to give her. That could come later.

"Hang on to this thought, darling," he murmured to her. "No matter what happens, I'll be here for you and the boy."

"You don't like children."

"I love your son." He couldn't hold in the words. "I didn't want to. I was afraid. To love someone meant I might be hurt again. I am hurting, Stacy. For you. For Billy. For myself. For all the years we might not get to spend together because I was too blind to see what life still offered."

Stacy laid her hand over his and stilled its movement against her face. "I can't think about that right now."

"I know." He kissed her palm, then held her hand in his lap. She felt his warmth flow around her.

Once she'd thought love would be like that—a steady warmth to keep a marriage going through the coldest of winters, with an occasional flare-up to keep things lively. She wasn't sure about that anymore, though.

"Don't give up," he said as if reading her mind.

"All right," she whispered.

Gareth prayed that her faith would be rewarded. If he could have moved heaven and earth to save her child, he would have. But all he could do was wait with her and tell her silently of his love.

Stacy was allowed to see Billy for a few minutes each hour. At dawn, she drank the tenth cup of coffee Gareth brought her.

The pediatrician returned before she finished it. "The medicine is in. The chief of pediatrics and the hospital board have given their approval to use it. We're ready."

Stacy felt Gareth's arm slide around her waist. She leaned against him. "Good," she said, drawing on his strength.

"You two can come into the room, but stay out of the way."

"We will," Gareth promised for both of them. He smiled at Stacy. "It'll be okay. Come on."

Together they followed the doctor into the ICU area. Billy was in an open incubator, a respirator hissing rhythmically close by. The heart monitor indicated a regular heartbeat.

The medical team stood ready. The doctor removed the IV and inserted the hypodermic needle. She slowly administered the drug. When she finished, she removed the respirator. They waited in total silence.

A second went by. Ten. Fifteen.

A shudder went through Billy's tiny body. His arms jerked. His fingers tightened. His legs kinked up, and his mouth dropped open. He drew a breath and let it out in a wail. His face turned an indignant red. He was breathing!

The seven adults laughed. The more he cried, the more they laughed. He stopped and gazed around.

Gareth pushed Stacy forward. She bent over her son and smiled. He smiled, then yawned as wide as his mouth would go. For the next three hours, he fussed and fretted. Stacy played with him. When that wouldn't do, Gareth walked the floor until his cries quietened.

At last, after he settled down enough to drink his fill of his mother's milk, his eyelids drooped and closed. He slept, looking perfectly peaceful and perfectly all right.

"The sleep of the innocent," Gareth murmured.

Thank you, God....

It was past nine. The hospital bustled as shifts changed and routines, suspended during the night, were resumed. Billy was doing fine. No signs of any trouble at all after the trauma.

Stacy sat beside the incubator, her hand constantly touching her son. She looked up and smiled. Fatigue showed itself in the lines between her eyes, the shadows beneath them.

Gareth's heart did a nosedive, righted itself and spun around dizzily. He'd forgotten what strange things love did to the human body. But he was willing to learn again.

That's what he wanted to tell Stacy. He understood why his proposal of marriage had hurt her. He'd offered reasons when she had wanted love. He'd wanted her, but he hadn't wanted to call it more than passion.

Stupid, really stupid. He could have lost her as easily as they had nearly lost her son. It was unthinkable. They were his, those two. She'd come to him to birth her son. Tha made him the surrogate father. He'd tell her so as soon as possible.

The pediatrician with the beautiful eyes of a Mona Lisa came in. She examined Billy and checked his reflexes. "He's right as rain," she declared. "You can take him home."

Stacy's eyes went big.

"You'll have a monitor like the one on him now. It sounds an alarm if he pulls another of those breath-holding tricks on us." Her smile was reassuring.

"He'll do fine," Gareth told Stacy. He meant to see to it. Eventually, they sorted through the checkout ritual and got on their way. Stacy sat in the back seat to be closer to Billy.

At the apartment, she carried the baby while Gareth brought up the monitoring equipment. The couple who lived across from Stacy opened their door just as they stepped out of the elevator. They took one look at him, then closed and locked their door.

Gareth chuckled.

Stacy flashed him a sparkling glance. "They probably think I've gotten mixed up with a madman. You're lucky they didn't call the police." The long hours of the night strayed into her eyes. "So am I. I couldn't have made it without you. Billy wouldn't have—"

"Hush," he admonished softly. "We'll talk later." He pushed open the door when she unlocked it and allowed her to precede him inside. Sixteen hours had passed since they were last there, but it seemed to him that it had been a lifetime.

He set up the monitoring equipment, checked to make sure it worked. It did. The alarm woke Billy, who started, then cried loudly. Smiling, Stacy picked him up and settled into the rocker-recliner. Gareth went to put on a pot of coffee while she nursed her child.

Later, when she came into the kitchen, he told her to go to bed. She shook her head.

"I couldn't sleep," she explained.

"You didn't sleep last night. I doubt if you'll sleep to-night, so you'll need some rest. I'll stay to make sure you don't sleep through the alarm or any of the other things that you're afraid might happen."

She tried to protest, but he insisted. At last she gave in and went off to shower and change into pajamas. He settled into the comfortable chair in the baby's room and read a magazine.

He thought over the revelations of the night. He stood and looked at the sleeping boy. This time when his heart tightened, he smiled. After patting the sleeping child, he resumed his vigil.

Stacy woke with a start. She sat up and frantically gazed around the tranquil bedroom. The apartment was silent. Her nightmare came back to haunt her. Fear sluiced down her back—cold, sweaty, mind-numbing.

"Billy." She flew out of bed, down the hall and into the baby's room.

She stopped just inside the door, her heart thudding. Relief left her weak and trembling.

Billy was there. Safe. Asleep. On Gareth's chest.

The rocker-recliner was tilted back as far as it would go. The monitoring equipment, mounted on an IV rack, stood sentinel beside them. Gareth's hands were laced together across the baby's bottom, holding the child securely in his grasp.

It was the most beautiful sight she'd ever seen.

Gareth opened his eyes. For a long minute, they watched each other without moving. Then he smiled.

It filled her with a radiance so bright, she could hardly stand it. She smiled, then she laughed. She skimmed across the floor to her two men.

Gazing into her eyes, Gareth saw the words weren't necessary. He'd say them later, but she knew. She knew....

Chapter Eleven

The month of June was the most perfect for weddings. The second Sunday dawned bright as a robin's egg. Stacy looked out the window of the Clelland home in Virginia and laughed softly.

Mrs. Clelland was directing the caterers, the florists, the minister, her husband, their guests and Gareth. Maudie sat in the front row, the bassinet in the aisle beside her, decked out in festive ribbons, which Billy persisted in trying to eat.

He would get a bite of wedding cake later.

"Ready?" She faced Pete and nodded. He held out his arm. She tucked her hand into it and walked outside.

The photographer snapped pictures while Shirl's pilot husband filmed the procedure. Stacy felt quite beautiful in her white silk suit with pink accessories.

And indescribably happy.

No one could be luckier than she was—a handsome husband, a perfect child and a cruise in the Mediterra

nean to all the places she'd read about. Italy, Greece, Tur-
key, Egypt, Spain, Portugal. She couldn't believe it.

Billy and Maudie would be with them in a separate room
across the parlor from the master suite. It was too wonderful.

Shirl, dressed in champagne silk with an Egyptian
necklace sparkling in the sun and long spiral earrings dan-
gling from her ears, stood at the end of the white satin
carpet. The music started. She gave Stacy a wink, then
walked with stately dignity down the aisle.

Stacy and Pete moved into place behind the matron of
honor. At last they came to the bower of flowers where
Gareth, his father and the minister waited. Her eyes widened.

When Gareth turned fully toward her, she saw he held
Billy in his arms. The love in his eyes made tears form in
hers. She sternly forced them back. No tears today, she
warned her shaky emotions.

She listened to her husband's voice and followed his
vows with her own. Billy was cradled securely against
Gareth's chest. And he squeezed her hand and held it
clasped in his after they exchanged rings.

At last it was finished. He bent over and kissed her.

Everyone clapped. Pete claimed a kiss from her while
Shirl did the same with Gareth. Shirl leaned against her
own husband and fanned her face. "I can see why you fell
or Gareth," she told Stacy in a stage whisper. "He's got
kiss like a twenty-mule team kick."

That brought more laughter. The afternoon passed in a
appy daze. Then it was time for them to go to the hon-
ymoon suite where they would spend their wedding night
efore beginning their trip.

Gareth went with her to the nursery quarters to change
othes and let her feed their son once more before they

left. There was extra milk in the freezer to get him through until morning.

"You're beautiful," he told her when she sat in the rocking chair in her slip while Billy tugged hungrily.

"You, too."

They smiled at each other.

"I can't wait for our next child. Dr. Kate says she'll let me do the delivery," he said, never taking his eyes from his bride and new son. "I figure about nine months from tonight..."

A blush suffused Stacy's cheeks. Tonight. It was what she'd been waiting for. Gareth, too. They'd already agreed they wanted another child as soon as may be.

"Me, too."

"A girl," he told her. "A bossy little sister for Billy. Someone to take my side of our arguments."

He looked so pleased, she had to smile. The big lummox, grinning like a politician on the campaign trail.

Stacy let her breath out in a deep sigh of happiness.

"Smile," Gareth ordered, producing a camera and proceeding to take several snapshots of her and Billy.

A picture of love, Stacy thought. She had many such pictures. There would be more. Of Billy on his birthdays. Fishing with his dad and grandfather. Sticking number tags on items for the annual auction for his grandmother. Making cookies with her and a sister or brother, or both someday.

"Ready?" Gareth asked when she finished and put Bill in the crib. His voice was deep, husky and very, very sexy.

"Yes."

He enfolded her in his arms after she had slipped into simple summer dress. Her breath snagged for a second when she saw the look in his eyes.

Tenderness. Love. Desire.

"A steady love," she murmured. "I always wanted a steady kind of love."

"It'll always be there for you," he promised.

He leaned over so he could hold her closer, his warmth pouring over her.

She laughed.

"I love it when you do that," he said, becoming serious. "When you laugh and look at me with love in your eyes." He nuzzled his face into her hair. "I never thought I'd have another love in my life...and then there were you and the baby, invading my mountain retreat, refusing to let me hibernate in my own self-pity, driving me crazy with longing—"

"I couldn't help but love you," she whispered. She batted her lashes at him. "When you helped me with Billy, I realized what a catch you were. All that valuable experience. Now when we have another child—"

His lips cut off the rest of the statement, but he finished it in his heart. *Our love will expand to include it, too.*

She'd come to his house to deliver a briefcase of law reviews. Instead, he'd had to do an unexpected delivery, one that ended up bringing him joy and happiness and peace. And the greatest love he'd ever known. It was a fair exchange.

* * * * *

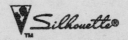

HE'S A FABULOUS FATHER...
TIMES TWO!

TWICE A FATHER
by
MOYRA TARLING
(SR #1156, June)

Shay O'Brien never expected to see Reeve Walker again—as a single dad, yet! She'd come home to start over with her own daughter, Mandy. Problem was, it wouldn't be long before Reeve discovered that their long-lost love had left Shay not just memories, but Mandy—who happened to be best friends with his child!

Don't miss TWICE A FATHER
by Moyra Tarling.

Available in June, only from

Silhouette
R O M A N C E™

**The wedding celebration was so nice...
too bad the bride wasn't there!**

Runaway Brides

Find out what happens when three brides have a change of heart.

Three complete stories by some of your favorite authors—all in one special collection!

YESTERDAY ONCE MORE
by Debbie Macomber

FULL CIRCLE
by Paula Detmer Riggs

THAT'S WHAT FRIENDS ARE FOR
by Annette Broadrick

Available this June wherever books are sold.

Look us up on-line at:http://www.romance.net

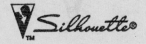

Silhouette®

SREQ696

"As the father of six adopted children,

I'm not your typical bachelor. But I may not stay one for long, now that I've met the woman of my dreams—Kristen Fielding. I can only hope she'll grow to love my kids as much as I do. Then I'll make her Mrs. Fernando Ibarra—and when she's the mother of my child, she'll say these words to me…"

HAPPY FATHER'S DAY
by
Barbara Faith
(SE #1033)

In June, Silhouette Special Edition brings you

That's My Baby!

Sometimes bringing up baby can bring surprises… and showers of love.

TMB696

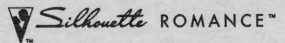

Silhouette ROMANCE™

is proud to present Carla Cassidy's
TWENTY-FIFTH book:

DADDY ON THE RUN
by
CARLA CASSIDY
(SR #1158, June)

Book four of her miniseries

Just when she was beginning to rebuild her life, Julianne Baker's
husband, Sam, was back! He had left only to protect her and their
little girl—but would Julianne be able to trust her husband's love
again, and give their family a second chance at happiness?

The Baker Brood: Four siblings in search of justice find love along
the way....

Don't miss the conclusion of **The Baker Brood** miniseries,
Daddy on the Run, available in June, only from

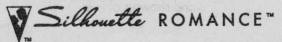

Silhouette ROMANCE™

BAKER4

This July, watch for the delivery of...

An exciting new miniseries that appears in a different Silhouette series each month. It's about love, marriage—and Daddy's unexpected need for a baby carriage!

Daddy Knows Last unites five of your favorite authors as they weave five connected stories about baby fever in New Hope, Texas.

- **THE BABY NOTION** by Dixie Browning
  (SD#1011, 7/96)

- **BABY IN A BASKET** by Helen R. Myers
  (SR#1169, 8/96)

- **MARRIED...WITH TWINS!**
  by Jennifer Mikels
  (SSE#1054, 9/96)

- **HOW TO HOOK A HUSBAND (AND A BABY)**
  by Carolyn Zane
  (YT#29, 10/96)

- **DISCOVERED: DADDY** by Marilyn Pappano
  (IM#746, 11/96)

Daddy Knows Last arrives in July...only from

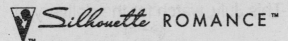
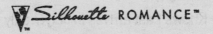